**Cara Colter** shares her life in beautiful British Columbia, Canada, with her husband, nine horses and one small Pomeranian with a large attitude. She loves to hear from readers, and you can learn more about her and contact her through Facebook.

### Books by Cara Colter

### Harlequin Romance

*The Vineyards of Calanetti*

*Soldier, Hero...Husband?*

*The Gingerbread Girls*

*Snowflakes and Silver Linings*

*Battle for the Soldier's Heart*
*Snowed in at the Ranch*
*Second Chance with the Rebel*
*How to Melt a Frozen Heart*
*Rescued by the Millionaire*
*The Millionaire's Homecoming*
*Interview with a Tycoon*
*Meet Me Under the Mistletoe*
*The Pregnancy Secret*
*Housekeeper Under the Mistletoe*
*The Wedding Planner's Big Day*
*Swept into the Tycoon's World*

Visit the Author Profile page
at Harlequin.com for more titles.

To Carol Geurts, who shows dignity, courage and integrity through all of life's storms. You are an inspiration.

## Praise for
## Cara Colter

"The story is filled with romantic scenes, from swimming lessons, to picnics and dancing under the stars. There's humor and laughter, there's pain and sorrow, but most of all, there's a love that heals the broken hearts, and brings these two lonely souls together."

—*Goodreads* on *Soldier, Hero...Husband?*

***Aidan was drinking in her face with a look she could not move away from.***

"Not beautiful," Noelle stammered. "I'm not."

"What would make you believe such a thing?"

Her mouth opened to begin reiterating a long list of proofs, but not a single sound came out.

Aidan took off his glove. He reached out with a gentleness that was so exquisite she felt she might cry for the confirmation of his truth in it. His hand warm, his skin silk over iron, touched her cheek, rested there. She could not move away from his touch, held there, captive to his unexpected tenderness.

"You are so beautiful," he said softly. "You may be the most beautiful woman I have ever seen."

Her mouth fell open. She could feel herself leaning toward whatever she saw in his eyes.

"Daddy, are you going to kiss Noelle?"

The little voice, inquisitive, delighted, yanked them apart.

His hand fell down. He shoved it into his pocket. "Of course not!" he said.

"No!" Noelle agreed.

But that near-miss, near-kiss moment was sizzling in the air between them.

Dear Reader,

Life has dealt me a few unexpected challenges in the past few years. Naturally, my initial reaction is indignation. What? I'm a good person. I don't deserve any bad luck, failure or bumps in the road.

But when I think about it, isn't an unexpected ill fortune, a gut-wrenching disappointment, a heartbreak at the very soul of every single story?

In real life, as well as in fiction, herein lies the turning point, the opportunity to be braver than I have ever been before and to explore life's unpredictability and fragility. I always seem to emerge from a challenging period humbled, but somehow more whole and more human.

I become more aware of simple gifts threaded through everyday life: sunlight spinning my dog's fur to gold, the comforting slosh of the dishwasher running, my partner throwing back his head and laughing.

I am more aware than ever of how the gift of a great story can provide respite from troubles and give hope of better days to come.

So, in this season of wonder, I give you this story, my Christmas gift to you. I wish you blessings and miracles and a heart that is open to receiving them.

With love,

*Cara*

# *Snowbound with the Single Dad*

### *Cara Colter*

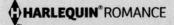

Recycling programs
for this product may
not exist in your area.

ISBN-13: 978-1-335-13540-7

Snowbound with the Single Dad

First North American publication 2018

Copyright © 2018 by Cara Colter

**Printed in U.S.A.**

# CHAPTER ONE

"THERE'S MY LITTLE Christmas star!"

Noelle felt a swell of joy as she watched her grandfather, Rufus, shut down the tractor and climb down off it. He paused to lift the old black Lab, Smiley, out of the cab. Then he turned and came through the snow toward her, Smiley shuffling behind him with his happy grin in place, despite the dog's pained gait.

She was relieved to see that, unlike Smiley, her grandpa was agile, surprisingly strong-looking for a man of seventy-eight years. He was dressed for cold, in a thick woolen toque, mittens and a lined plaid lumber jacket.

His embrace, too, was powerful as he came and hugged her tight, lifting her right off her feet.

He put her down and regarded her. "You haven't been losing weight, have you?"

"No," she said quickly, although she wasn't at all certain. She had always been a slight girl, but she hadn't been near a weigh scale since the abrupt end of her engagement. Noelle was fairly certain you could not lose weight eating chocolate ice cream for supper. And also, sometimes, for breakfast.

Their worry was mutual. It was to be their first Christmas without Grandma McGregor. In those months after Grandma had died, there had been something in her grandpa's voice on the phone, which Noelle had not heard before—a weariness, a disconnect, as if he was not quite there. Sometimes he had made mistakes about what day it was, and seemed confused about other small details of daily life. Other times he had reminisced so obsessively about the past that Noelle had been convinced he was declining, too, dying of a broken heart.

Then, a few weeks ago, she had noticed an improvement. To her great surprise and relief, he'd actually seemed excited about Christmas. It had always been such a magical time of year in her family, partly because it was her birthday, too. Would it be too much to expect a Christmas miracle that would begin to heal their losses this year?

But when Noelle had driven into the yard and seen her grandpa had not put up a single decoration, she had felt her heart fall. Then, when she had noticed the tractor tracks, heading off into nowhere, she'd been frightened.

He didn't have cattle anymore. Where was he going? She'd followed along the tracks with great trepidation.

"Grandpa." She sighed, feeling that sense of coming home. She got down on her knees and gave Smiley a long hug and an ear scratching before she got up and surveyed her grandfather's project.

He seemed to be clearing snow in a large square in the middle of what used to be a cow pasture. "What on earth are you doing?"

His arm looped over her shoulder, he turned and looked with pleasure at his handiwork.

"I'm building me a helicopter landing pad," he said, and her sense of well-being plummeted.

"A what?" she stammered.

"You heard me. Don't go giving me that have-you-lost-your-mind look. Come on, we'll go to the house and have coffee. You brought everything you need for a nice Christmas at the ranch?"

She thought he might want to take the tractor back to the house, but instead he turned with her and walked the pounded-down snow of the tractor track, Smiley dogging their heels.

"Yes." Noelle hesitated, and then asked, "I wondered why you didn't have any decorations up yet?"

"I thought it would be good to do it together."

Even though she had never helped with things like putting the outside lights up, she loved the idea of them working together to re-create Christmases like the ones they had always enjoyed.

"That sounds fun. I'm so looking forward to the break. I'll be here now until just after New Year's."

"Ah, good. Good. Everybody else will leave Boxing Day, so we'll have a bit of time for just you and me."

"What do you mean everybody?" she asked, surprised.

"Oh, my goodness, Ellie," he said, calling her by his pet name for her, "wait until I show you what I've gone and done. Have you ever heard of Me-Sell?"

She cocked her head at him quizzically.

"You know, the place on the interstate where you put the ads up?"

"The internet? Oh, you mean I-Sell? That huge online classified ad site?"

"That's it!"

The thought of her grandpa on I-Sell gave her pause. He still heated his house with wood. He received two channels on his old television set—if he fiddled with the rabbit ears on top of it long enough. He did not own a cell phone, not that there was signal anywhere near here. He and Grandma had never had a computer, never mind the internet.

"I go down to the library in the village and use the interstate," he said.

"Internet," she corrected him weakly.

"Whatever. I decided to sell some of my old machines out in the barn. Just taking up space. Ed down the road got a pretty penny for his. He did it all on I-Sell."

"Do you need money?" she asked, appalled that somehow this had passed her by in their weekly telephone conversations. She got out here to visit him at least once a month. Why hadn't she noticed he was pinching his pennies? Had her own double heartbreak made her that self-involved?

"Good grief, no! Got more money than I know what to do with since I sold off most of the land except for this little parcel around the home place."

Another of the recent heartbreaking losses had been that decision to sell off most of the land that had been in the McGregor family for generations. There was no one left to work it. In her fantasies, Noelle had hoped one day she and Mitchell would buy it back.

They came over a little rise, and both of them paused. There it sat, the home place, prettier than a Christmas card. Surrounded by mounds of white snow was a large two-story house, pale yellow with deep indigo shutters, a porch wrapping around the whole lower floor, smoke chugging out the rock chimney.

If her grandmother had been alive, the house would have been decorated by now, December 21. There would have been lights along the roofline and a huge wreath on the front door, the word *HOPE* peeking out from under a big red bow. The huge blue spruce in the front yard would have been dripping with lights. But this year there was not a single decoration, and it made Noelle's eyes smart, even if her grandfather had waited for her to do it.

Behind the house was a barn, once red, now mostly gray. In the near distance the foothills, snow dusted, rolled away from them, and in the far distance the peaks of the Rockies were jagged and white against a bright blue sky.

They passed the barn on the way to the house, and two large gray horses with feathered feet and dappled rumps came running out of a paddock behind it.

"Hello, Fred, hello, Ned," she said affectionately.

Noelle went over to the fence and held out her hand. Fred blew a warm cloud of moist air onto her hand. She reached up to touch his nose, but just as she did, a tiny little horse, as black as Smiley, exploded through the snow from behind the barn, and the other two took off, snorting and blowing.

The tiny horse, having successfully chased away the competition, strained its neck to reach over the fence, and nipped at where her fingers dangled.

She snatched them away, and the pony gave an indignant shake of its scruffy black mane and charged off in the direction it had come.

"Who—or what—is that?" she asked.

"That's Gidget," her grandfather said. "She seems like a nasty little piece of work, but you'd be surprised how hard it is to find a pony close to Christmas."

"A pony for Christmas?"

Noelle shot her grandfather a look. Again, she had the terrifying thought her grandfather might be slipping, that maybe he thought she was a little girl again.

"She's a Christmas surprise."

"Oh! You're keeping someone's surprise pony until Christmas?"

"Something like that. Look at you shivering. City gal."

He took his toque off, revealing a head of very thick silver hair. He placed it on her own head and pulled it tenderly over her ears, as if she was, indeed, twelve again and not twenty-three. This time, instead of terrifying her, the casual gesture made her feel deeply loved.

He moved to her car, an economy model that had struggled a bit on the very long, snowy road that led to his place from the secondary highway. Her grandfather wrestled her suitcase out of the trunk. It was a big suitcase, filled with gifts and warm clothes, and her skates. The pond behind the house would be frozen over. The suitcase had wheels, but her grandpa chose to carry it and Noelle knew better than to insult him by offering to help.

When they walked in the back door into the back porch, the smell of coffee was strong in the house, though she immediately missed the just-out-of-the-oven aroma of her grandmother's Christmas baking.

They shrugged out of jackets and boots, and left the suitcase there. Noelle pulled off her grandfather's toque and smoothed her hair in the mirror. Her faintly freckled cheeks and nose were already pretty pink from being outside, but she knew herself to be an unremarkable woman. Mouse-brown hair, shoulder-length, straight as spaghetti, eyes that were neither brown nor blue but some muddy moss color in between, pixie-like features that could be made cute— not beautiful—with makeup, not that she bothered anymore.

The dog had already settled in his bed by the wood heater when she got into the kitchen. While her grandfather added wood to the heater, Noelle looked around with fondness.

The kitchen was nothing like the farmhouse kitchens that were all the rage in the home-decorating magazines right now. It had old, cracked linoleum on the floor, the paint was chipping off cabinets and the counters were cluttered with everything from engine pieces to old gloves. The windows were abundant but old, glazed over with frost inside the panes.

Aside from the fact that her grandmother would not have tolerated those engine pieces on the counter, and would have had some Christmas decorations up, Noelle felt that sigh of homecoming intensify within her.

Her grandfather and grandmother had raised her when her parents had died in an automobile accident when she was twelve. In all the world, this kitchen was the place she loved the most and felt the safest.

"Tell me about the helicopter pad," she said, taking a seat at the old table. The coffee had been brewing on the woodstove, and her grandfather plopped a mug down in front of her. She took a sip, and her eyes nearly crossed it was so strong. She reached hastily for the sugar pot.

"Well, it really started when I was watching

the news one night." He took the seat across the table from her and regarded her with such unabashed affection that it melted her heart and the intensity of that feeling *home* grew.

"There was this story about this girl—not here, mind, England or Vancouver—"

Both equally foreign places to her grandfather.

"—who was going to be all alone for Christmas, so she just put an ad on something like I-Sell and all these people answered her, and she chose a family to have Christmas with."

Her grandfather was beaming at her as if this fully explained the helicopter pad he was building in his cow pasture.

"Go on."

"So I was on there anyway, trying to figure out how to put up a posting for my old junk in the barn, and I just had this thought that I missed Christmas the way it used to be."

"You and me and Grandma?" she said wistfully, thinking of music and baking and decorating, and neighbors dropping by.

"Even before that. You know, TV was late coming to these parts. It was better without it. And a whole lot better without the interstate."

No point telling him again. Noelle waited.

"Don't even get me going on what cell phones are doing to the world."

"I won't," Noelle said, though in truth she knew it wouldn't be long before she missed all her social media platforms. Or more to the point, relentlessly and guiltily spying on someone else's newly exciting life through their prolific postings.

"We used to have big gatherings at Christmas," her grandfather said longingly. "When I was a boy, on Christmas Day the whole community would show up at the old hall, and there would be a Christmas concert, and dinner, and games. Those tables would be groaning under the weight of turkeys and hams and bowls of mashed spuds and pies. Oh, the pies! The women would try to outdo themselves on pies.

"People sang, and talked together. They exchanged gifts with their neighbors. Not much, you see, a homemade whistle, a flour sack, bleached white and embroidered with something nice, like *Bless This House*. If you knew a family that was having a rough go, you made sure all the kids had a present, and that they got a big fat ham to take home."

Noelle's sense of worry was gnawing at her again. As lovely a picture as he was painting, her grandfather had never been like this. Grandma had pretty much looked after Christmas, he'd done the outside decorating and hitched up the old horses for the mandatory

Christmas sleigh ride, usually after much nagging! Until Grandma had died, he had never been given to reminiscing. He was pragmatic, not sentimental!

"So," he said, "I got me an email address and I just put a little ad on there, inviting people to an old-fashioned Christmas, if they wanted one."

"Here?" Noelle asked, stunned.

"Well, sure. Can you think of a better place?"

"Grandpa, you can't invite strangers off the internet to your home!"

He folded his arms across his plaid shirt. His craggy face got a stubborn look on it. "Well, too late for your good advice, little miss Dear Abby, I already done it."

"People replied?"

"All kinds of them," he said with satisfaction.

"But how do you know if they're good people?" Noelle asked. Was that faint hysteria in her voice?

Her grandfather patted her hand. "Oh, Noelle, most folks are good. You've just lost a little faith because of that fella, Michael—"

"Mitchell," she corrected him weakly. She did not want to think of that "fella" with his newly exciting life right now!

"Does this have something to do with the helicopter pad?" she whispered, full of trepidation.

"Yup, indeed. Some kind of Mr. Typhoon is coming here."

"Tycoon?" she asked, despite herself.

"Whatever."

"Oh, Grandpa!"

"With his little girl, who lost her mommy."

"Grandpa! Tell me you didn't send anyone any money."

"Well, I did send somebody money. Not the typhoon, someone else. They wanted to come to my Old-Fashioned Country Christmas, but my goodness, them people have had a run of bad luck. Couldn't even put together the money for a tank of gasoline."

Noelle felt sick. How far had this gone? How many people had duped him out of his money? Her hopes for a healing Christmas were evaporating.

Her grandpa was an absolute innocent in the high-tech world. All kinds of people out there were just waiting to prey on a lonely old man; all kinds of villains were trolling the internet to find the likes of her grandfather. She hoped he hadn't spouted off to anyone else about having more money than he could use.

"Grandpa," she said gently. "It's a hoax. If the *tycoon* hasn't asked you for money yet, he will. You're probably being scammed..."

Her grandfather was scowling at her. "It ain't like that."

"How do you know?"

"Because they sent me this." He produced a piece of paper from a heap of papers leaning off one of the counters. Noelle took it and stared at it. It appeared to be specs for building a rudimentary helicopter pad.

"Oh, no, Grandpa," she said. This was how easy it was to fool an old man. The drawing could have been done by a child.

Her grandfather cocked his head.

"Hear that?" he asked triumphantly.

She stared at him. She heard absolutely nothing. She felt the most heartbreaking sadness. What a year of losses. The land. Her grandmother. Then, weeks after her grandmother had passed, her fiancé announcing he just wasn't "ready." To commit. To live in one place. Apparently to hold down a job in the oil industry that had employed them both. Mitchell had gone off to Thailand to "find himself."

If his favorite social media page was any indication, he seemed to be being helped in this pursuit by a bevy of exotic-looking, bikini-clad beauties who had made Noelle newly aware of her lack of boldness—she had never worn a bikini—plus her own plainness and her paleness.

So, she had lost her family ranch, her grandmother and her fiancé. It was true she had held on to hope for a ridiculously long period of time that Mitchell would come to his senses and come back, even after his final betrayal.

But now, this felt as if it would be the final blow, if she was losing her grandfather, only in quite a different way. His mind going, poor old guy. She'd heard of this before. Moments of lucidity interspersed with, well, this.

He had pushed back from the table and was hurrying to the door.

"I can't not be there when they land," he said eagerly. "And I better throw some hay at that pony, so she's on the back side of the barn. Don't want that secret out yet."

Even the dog looked doubtful, and not very happy to be going back outside.

"Grandpa," she said soothingly, getting up, "come sit down. You can help me take my suitcase up. Maybe we'll go find a tree this afternoon, put up some decorations—"

Her grandfather was ignoring her. He laced up his boots and went out the door, the reluctant dog on his heels. Moments later his side-by-side all-terrain vehicle roared to life and pulled away, leaving an almost eerie silence in its wake.

And then she heard it.

The very distinctive wop-wop-wop of a helicopter in the distance.

She dashed to the back porch, put on her grandfather's toque, grabbed her jacket, shoved boots on her feet and raced out the door.

# CHAPTER TWO

"KEEP BACK FROM IT!" her grandfather shouted over his shoulder.

Noelle arrived at the landing pad, breathless from running. The blades of the helicopter were throwing up so much snow that for a moment Noelle lost sight of her grandfather, the dog and the helicopter.

And then the engines died, and the snow settled, and it was very quiet. She peered at the helicopter. It was a burnished gold color, wrapped in a word, *Wrangler.*

Behind the bubble of a window, she could see a man doing something at the controls. He had a shock of dark hair falling over his brow, a strong profile and aviator-style sunglasses. From this distance she couldn't make out his features, and yet, somehow she knew—perhaps from his chosen entry—that everything about this man would be extraordinary.

As she watched, he took off the earphones

he was wearing and the sunglasses, which he folded into his front breast pocket. He got out his door with an easy leap. He acknowledged Noelle and her grandfather with a slight raise of his hand and then moved to the passenger door.

He was wearing a brown distressed-leather pilot's jacket lined with sheepskin. His shoulders appeared impossibly broad, and dark slacks accentuated the long lines of powerful legs. He moved with the innate grace of a man extremely confident in himself.

Noelle could see now his hair was more than dark, black and shiny as a raven's wing. His features were strong and even, with the faintest hint of whisker shadowing on the hollows of his cheeks and on that merest hint of a cleft at his chin. He glanced toward her, and she felt the jolt of his eyes: electric blue, cool, assessing.

And ever so vaguely familiar. Noelle stared at his face, wondering where she had seen him before, and then stunned recognition dawned. Why wouldn't he be confident in himself?

Aidan Phillips was even more of a presence in real life than he was in pictures. And there were plenty of pictures of him.

Less so now than a few years ago, when he and his wife, Sierra, had been unofficially crowned Canadian royalty, he an oil industry magnate, and she a renowned actress. Every public second of their romance and subsequent marriage had been relentlessly documented, photographed and commented on, as if their coming together was Canada's answer to a real-life fairy tale.

Without, sadly, the happy ending.

"Do you know who that is?" she asked her grandfather in an undertone.

He lifted a shoulder.

"He's one of the richest men in Canada."

"I told you," Rufus said, triumphantly. "A typhoon. Though it's a poor man, indeed, who thinks all it takes to be rich is money. Ask her."

"Ask who?"

"Her."

Noelle turned back to see Aidan lifting a little girl out of the helicopter passenger seat. Of course, she knew he was a widower, and she knew there was a child, but he used his substantial influence to protect his daughter from any kind of public exposure.

The little girl was gorgeous—wild black curls springing from under a soft pink, very fuzzy hat that matched her jacket and leggings and snow boots. The cutest little pink furry muff dangled from a string out the sleeve of her jacket. She had the same electric blue eyes as her father. Noelle guessed her to be about five.

Aidan Phillips set the child down in the snow,

and she looked around. Smiley ambled over, and the little girl squealed with delight and got down on both chubby knees, throwing her arms around the dog.

"Don't let him lick your face," a shrill voice commanded.

A third passenger was being helped out of the helicopter, an elderly woman with a pinched, forbidding expression.

"Well," Grandpa said, too loudly. "There's a face that would make a train take a dirt road."

"Grandpa!"

But her grandpa had moved forward to greet his guests. After a moment he waved her up, and Noelle went forward, feeling the absolute awkwardness of the situation.

"And this is my granddaughter, Noelle, born on Christmas Day."

Noelle cringed inwardly. Was her grandfather going to reveal her whole history?

"We just call her Ellie, though."

Actually, no one but her grandfather called her Ellie anymore, but she felt it would be churlish to correct him.

"This is Tess and Aidan," her grandfather said, as if he was introducing people he had known for a long time.

Despite her feeling of being caught off balance, Noelle smiled at the child, before turning her attention to the man. He extended his hand, and she ripped off her mitten and found her hand enveloped in one that was strong and warm. Ridiculously, she wished she was not in a parka nearly the same shade of pink as the little girl's. She also wished for just the faintest dusting of makeup.

A woman would have to be dead—not merely heartbroken—to not want to make some sort of first impression on Aidan Phillips!

Still, she saw a faint wariness in those intense blue eyes as they narrowed on her face. When his hand enveloped hers it felt as if she had stood too close to lightning. She was tingling!

"A pleasure," he said, but there was something as guarded in his voice as in his eyes, and Noelle was fairly certain he did not think it was a pleasure at all. In fact, his voice was a growl of pure suspicion that sent a shiver up and down her spine. She snatched her hand away from his, put her mitten on and stepped back from him.

"This is quite a surprise," she stammered. "My grandfather only just told me we were having guests for Christmas."

"Nor did he tell me about the lovely granddaughter."

There was something about the way he said *lovely* that was faintly sarcastic, and Noelle felt an embarrassing blush rise up her cheeks. But then she realized Aidan was not commenting on the plainness she had become more painfully aware of since Mitchell's departure, but something else entirely.

Was Aidan Phillips insinuating her grandfather was matchmaking?

How dare he? If ever there was a person incapable of ulterior motives, it was Grandpa.

On the other hand—she slid her grandfather a look from under her lashes—was there a remote possibility he was meddling in her life? It seemed unlikely. Her grandfather was not a romantic. But he had been unabashed in his disapproval of her relationship with Mitchell, especially when they had moved in together.

Her relationship with Mitchell? Or just Mitchell as a person?

If her grandfather was matchmaking, he seemed rather indifferent to the first encounter of the lovebirds.

Realistically, it simply wasn't Grandpa's style. At all. And yet even as she thought that, she remembered bringing Mitchell to the ranch to meet her grandparents.

*What's wrong with him?* she had heard Grandpa ask her grandmother. *He doesn't act like he's the luckiest man in the world. He doesn't seem to know how beautiful she is.*

Noelle had heard her grandmother's answer.
She knew she had. But every time she tried to
recall it, it flitted just beyond where her memory could find it, a wary bird that did not want
to be captured.

Her grandfather didn't even know about the
final betrayal: that Mitchell had emptied out
their joint bank account.

*I made it,* he'd said, when she had sent him
a frantic message through a social media mes-
saging service, asking where the money was.

There had been no acknowledgment that her
salary, which had taken care of bills and grocer-
ies, had allowed *them* to save quite a substantial nest egg. Toward a wedding. And a house.

What had Grandpa said when she had shown
up on his doorstep, her face swollen after a week
of solid crying? *It was better in the old days
when your family helped you find your partner.*

What was it with her grandfather and this
sudden sentimental attachment to how things
used to be?

Not that there was anything sentimental on
his face at the moment. He was scowling at the
older lady, who was wiping frantically at the
little girl's dog-kissed face with a linen hand-
kerchief.

"And I ain't had the pleasure?"

"Bertanana Sutton," she said regally, pausing

her wiping of the girl's face, but not standing and offering her hand, which Rufus seemed to take as an insult.

"Bertanana?" her grandfather repeated. "That's a mouthful."

"We just call her Nana, though," the little girl said, mischievously.

Grandpa guffawed loudly.

"Excuse me?" Bertanana said imperiously.

"Nana. Just like the Newfoundland dog in *Peter Pan*," Grandpa said.

First of all, Noelle was shocked that her grandfather knew anything about *Peter Pan*, let alone the name and breed of the dog. And second, why was he being so unforgivably rude?

Not that she needed to intervene. Nana was giving her grandfather a look that would have felled a lesser man—or made a train take a dirt road!

"Mrs. Sutton to you," she said.

He flinched and Noelle saw what the problem was. He'd felt judged at Nana's first insinuation that the dog—and its kisses—were dirty. Noelle had a terrible feeling this would not go well.

"Luggage?" Grandpa asked stiffly.

Aidan turned away from them and began to unload the helicopter. For a man who was CEO of a very large company, and moved in the rarefied circles of the very rich and very famous, he seemed every bit as strong as her grandfather. How was that possible when her grandfather was a hardworking man of the land?

With no conversation between them, Aidan and her grandfather filled the back of the side-by-side with quite a large number of suitcases and parcels, and then in went the dog, and Nana and Tess.

"Out of room," Grandpa said, happily, his hurt feelings put aside for now. He took the driver's seat. "You two will have to walk." And then he roared away with a wave of his hand, leaving her standing there in a cloud of snow with Aidan Phillips.

It was obvious there was no room on that vehicle. It made sense that Noelle and Aidan would be left to walk, being neither the youngest nor the oldest of the group.

And yet if someone was looking for evidence of an ulterior motive, it would seem almost embarrassingly obvious that her grandfather had engineered an opportunity to throw them together, alone.

Aidan shoved his hands deep in his pockets and gazed off at the snow-capped mountains, something tight and closed in his face.

She could smell the leather of his jacket in the cold air, and a faint and seductive scent, subtle as only the most expensive of colognes managed to be.

"I'm having a bit of trouble getting my head around all this," she said, her voice strained.

"As am I," he returned coolly.

"I'm not going to pretend I don't know who you are, though I suspect my grandfather doesn't have a clue. I work in Clerical for a small oil company in Calgary, so I know the basics of who is who in the oil industry. I know you are the CEO of the Calgary-based Wrangler Oil."

"And that I was married to Sierra Avanguard?" he asked quietly, his gaze disconcertingly direct on her face.

"Of course, that, too."

"I don't want any pictures of Tess showing up on social media," he said. "Or anywhere else."

It was said formidably, an order.

Really, was it unreasonable? He didn't know her. He was just laying the ground rules. But he was also her grandfather's guest, and it seemed a breach of her grandfather's hospitality for Aidan to feel it was necessary to say this.

"That's fine," she said, matching his cool tone. "I don't want any pictures of my grandfather surfacing, either. I'm sure his privacy is as important to him as yours is to you."

He looked stunned. Obviously, if he had ever

been put in his place before, it had been a long time ago.

He tilted his head at her, and looked a little more deeply. Reluctant amusement tickled around the line of that sinfully sensual mouth and sparked in his eyes for a second.

"Maybe he should stay off I-Sell, then," he suggested.

"My grandfather does not have a clue what the repercussions of putting his invitation in a virtual world could be," Noelle said. "I'm afraid I would have dissuaded him, had he confided his Old-Fashioned Country Christmas plans in me."

"Ah."

Noelle wondered if she should tell him there might be others coming. But were there? She decided to take her grandfather aside and find out whether, apart from sending money to strangers, he had any other confirmed guests, before setting off alarm bells. Besides, wasn't there a possibility this was between Aidan and Rufus and she should stay out of it?

Meanwhile she had to satisfy her curiosity about how Aidan Phillips had come to be standing in a field on her grandfather's property! Handsome men did not just fall from the heavens!

"I must say," Noelle said cautiously, "that you hardly seem like the type of man who would be searching an online ad site to make your Christmas plans."

"Oh? What type of man do I seem like?"

"The kind who would have a zillion much more glamorous Christmas options and invitations than this one."

"That's true," he said, with a sigh that could be interpreted as regretful that he had not accepted one of his many other invitations.

"So what brings you to Rufus McGregor's ranch for Christmas?" she pressed.

Aidan blew out a long breath and ran a gloved hand through his hair, scattering dark wisps that drifted like feathers before they settled obediently back into place. Such a small thing to find so utterly and disconcertingly sexy.

Her ex-fiancé, Mitchell, had been bald as a billiard ball.

It was the novelty of all that silky touchable-looking hair, she told herself firmly. But still, she had *noticed*. Not just noticed. No, noticed *and* found it attractive. This had to be nipped in the bud, of course.

Noelle closed her eyes for a moment. She summoned a picture in her mind of a red dress. It hung in her dark closet at home, its color dulled behind a plastic wrapper. It was the most glorious—and the most expensive—item of clothing she had ever owned.

She had bought it for the engagement party that had never happened. Now, she would never wear it. Or get rid of it, either. It would be defense against such things as this—an odd twinge of longing that had attacked without warning, the first such longing since Mitchell had packed a single bag—he'd only needed shorts and T-shirts for his new life, after all—and bid her adieu with undisguised eagerness to be gone.

"Are you all right?"

She opened her eyes. Aidan was looking at her quizzically.

"Yes, of course. I'm fine. You were going to tell me—"

He looked at her, considering. Something softened marginally in his expression. It was probably very obvious her discomfort was authentic, and that *if* her grandpa had something up his sleeve, she had had no part in it.

"How I came to be here?" he asked, his tone rueful.

She nodded.

"Never tell a five-nearly-six-year-old she can have anything she wants for Christmas."

# CHAPTER THREE

"SHE PICKED THIS?" Noelle asked, shocked. "Your daughter, Tess, could have anything she wanted for Christmas and she picked my grandfather's old place in the middle of nowhere?"

"Almost anything," Aidan clarified. "No pony."

*Uh-oh*. Did that explain nasty little Gidget's arrival on the ranch? Her grandfather *had* said it was the secret he didn't want let out yet.

"And no puppy," Aidan added after a moment. "I actually was foolish enough to say, in a moment of utter weakness, that she could have anything else."

Noelle suspected he had been momentarily so caught up in the guilt of refusing Tess a pony or a puppy that he had caved easily on her request to come here. But why had she wanted to come here?

"And she picked this?" Noelle asked again.

"I'm as flabbergasted as you are." He regarded her thoughtfully. "What do you think a little girl who could have anything would choose?"

Her opinion really seemed to matter to him. He was looking at her with discomfiting intensity. She hoped he wouldn't run his hand through his hair again.

"Disneyland?" she hazarded, after a moment's thought.

He looked disappointed in the answer, and she was annoyed with herself for feeling that she had not wanted to let him down.

"Yes, Disneyland. According to my research staff, the number one wish of children around the world is to visit a Disney resort."

She had not only disappointed, she hadn't even been original. Still, if for a moment she didn't make it all about her, what did it say about him that he had set his research staff on the task of discovering what would make his daughter's dreams come true?

"So, you took her?"

"Yes. Tess declared, at the top of her lungs, lying on the walkway in the middle of the park, *It is not Christmas without snow*," he informed Noelle solemnly. "Even though I explained to her the very first Christmas would not have had any snow, we were, at that point, beyond rational explanations.

"I'm lucky I wasn't arrested. Fortunately,

four-year-old meltdowns are not the unusual in 'the Happiest Place on Earth.'"

She had to bite back a desire to laugh at the picture forming in her mind of this self-contained man being held hostage by a four-year-old having a tantrum.

He went on, "The holiday transformation of *It's a Small World* failed to impress my daughter, despite the addition of fifty thousand Christmas lights, which is also the number of times I think we went through that particular attraction. For weeks after, I had 'Jingle Bells' and 'Deck the Halls' jangling away inside my head."

"Oh, dear," Noelle murmured. "Would you like me to take those off the caroling list?"

"There's to be caroling?" Aidan asked, horrified.

"All part of an old-fashioned Christmas," she said, deadpan. Of course, she had not planned a single thing for an old-fashioned Christmas. Was it wrong to take such delight in his discomfort? "I think it's a requirement, as well as snow. You can see we have plenty of that."

"The Christmas before Disneyland we had snow," he confessed. "My team found a place in the Finnish Lapland. We stayed in a glass igloo and witnessed the Northern Lights. We rode in a cart pulled by reindeer. We visited Santa's house."

"That sounds absolutely magical." Noelle actually was not sure anything her grandfather could offer would compete with such a Christmas.

"It does, doesn't it?"

"Oh, dear, I can tell by your tone—"

He nodded. "Another Christmas fail. She was three at the time. Santa was not as depicted in her favorite storybook. I think *creepy* is the word she used in reference to him. *Cweepy.* Rhotacism is perfectly normal until age eight."

"Rhotacism?" Noelle asked weakly.

"Trading out the *R* sound for *W*."

Which meant he had checked. Or his research staff had. It was all a bit sad, and somehow made him more dangerous than his wisps of dark hair falling gently back into place after he had raked his hand through them.

Before she could reconjure the red dress, he continued. "And the reindeer were a major letdown. Non-fliers. None with a red nose."

"I guess some elements of Christmas might be best left to the imagination," Noelle said. It seemed to her that Aidan, in his feverish efforts to manufacture the Christmas experience, might have missed the meaning of that first Christmas entirely.

She saw, again, just a hint of vulnerability in him—the single dad trying desperately to make his daughter happy. Especially at Christmas. Desperate enough to join strangers…

Noelle searched her memory. His wife had been a very famous and extraordinarily beautiful actress. Hadn't she died around Christmas? Three years ago? The papers had not been able to get enough of that sad little toddler's face. And then, to his credit, Aidan Phillips had managed to get his daughter out of the limelight and keep her out of it.

She could feel herself softening toward him the tiniest bit.

"And then you would think you could salvage Christmas with lovely gifts, wouldn't you?" He sighed with long-suffering.

Again, she felt he was missing the point, but she went along. "Aren't gifts for little girls easy? Hair ribbons and teddy bears and new pajamas? A jangly bracelet? A miniature oven?"

"Oh, right," Aidan said, as if Noelle was hopelessly naive.

Of course, his little girl probably got those things as a matter of course, so what did Tess then have to look forward to?

"Doesn't she tell you what she wants?"

"Yes, a puppy. And a pony. Every other item on her wish list is reserved for *Santa*. The fat happy Santa at the mall, not the skinny fellow in odd clothes with a real beard in Finland. And it's a secret. If you tell anyone, then Santa won't bring it to you, because the hearty laugh and twinkly eyes are just fronts for a mean-spirited old goat that would punish a little girl for telling her dad what she *really* wants."

Noelle was struck by an irony here. Aidan Phillips, one of the most wealthy and successful men in Canada, if not the world, was in hopelessly over his head when it came to being a daddy at Christmas.

What had her grandfather just said? That a man who thought money was the only way to be rich was very poor indeed?

Still, it seemed like it should all be fairly easy. Was he the kind of man who could complicate a dot?

"How about that line of dolls that is such a big hit? Millie something?"

"Jilly," he corrected her. "Jilly Jamjar. And her friends. Corrinne Cookiejar. Pauline Picklejar. They all come with the 'jar' they live in."

"Are you making this up?"

"Really? Do I look like the kind of man who could make up a line of dolls who live in jar houses?"

"No," she had to admit, "you do not."

"I wish I was making it up. She already has the first three in the series. But then along came Jerry. Jerry Juicejar."

It was quite funny listening to this extremely sophisticated man discuss the Jar dolls, fluent in their ridiculous names, but she had the feeling it would be a mistake to laugh.

"The Jarheads—my name for the toy manufacturers, not their own—in all their wisdom, made a limited edition of dear Jerry. There's a few thousand of him. Period. For millions of children screaming his name in adulation. I swear the Jarheads are in cahoots with the mean-spirited Santa.

"Which brings us to I-Sell. One momentary lapse on my part. *Okay, go ahead, see if you can find a Jerry Juicejar on there.*"

"You let your five-year-old daughter go on the internet?"

Noelle was treated to a flinty look of pure warning. *Do not judge me.*

"She's not five going on six, she's five going on twenty-one."

Which Noelle found terribly sad. Really, Tess was little more than a baby, only a year ago being quite capable of throwing a tantrum in the middle of a theme park. Still, she refrained from saying anything. She was beginning to suspect that the do-not-judge-me look she saw in his eyes had something to do with the fact that he had already judged himself with horrendous harshness.

"Plus, she wasn't by herself. Nana was supervising. I've got two acquisitions assistants looking for him full time, and they have not found anyone willing to part with a Jerry. There are some things," Aidan said with a miffed sigh, "that money can't buy."

"There are all kinds of things money can't buy," Noelle said firmly.

He looked dubious about that, even after his failed attempts to purchase Christmas happiness for his daughter with lavish holiday plans, research teams and acquisitions assistants.

"Is it possible Tess would like to just stay home for Christmas?" she suggested softly, as gently as she could. "She just wants what any child wants. To be with you. To be with her family."

"I'm it for family," he said tightly. "Me and Nana. Another fail in the Christmas department, I'm sure. And we don't stay home for Christmas."

*A fire*, Noelle seemed to remember. In their apartment? Christmas morning? A nation pulled from their Christmas joy to mourn with that very famous family.

"Anyway, she was looking for Jerry Juicejar, and what did she find while her supervisor nodded off on the sofa? An Old-Fashioned Country Christmas."

"You're quite lucky that's all she found," Noelle said.

Again, she got the flinty look, but underneath it she saw just a flicker of the magnitude of his sense of drowning in the sea of parenting requirements.

"You couldn't dissuade her?" She deliberately made her tone neutral, vigilantly nonjudgmental.

Not that he seemed to appreciate her effort! He shot her a look. "You'll soon see how easy it is to dissuade Tess. And I did, very foolishly, promise her she could have anything. A promise is a promise. She'll be the first to let you know that, too. She has a book by that title that she carries in her hip pocket for reference and reminder purposes. So be very careful what you tell her."

"I've made a note," she said seriously, and he shot her a suspicious look to see if she was making light of him.

"I had…er…some of my staff make sure your grandfather was legitimate."

It was faintly insulting, and yet she could hardly blame him.

"And then I spoke to your grandfather on the phone and it all seemed aboveboard. Nice old guy, first Christmas alone. Of course, he neglected to mention Ellie-born-on-Christmas-Day."

"Maybe your research teams just aren't that good," she said drily. "They can't find out what a little girl wants for Christmas and they totally missed me. I go by Noelle, actually, and being born on Christmas Day was not an indictable offense the last time I checked."

"Did I say it like it was?"

"You did."

"It's just so darn...cute. Most people, of course, would hate having their birthday over-shadowed by the 'big' day, but I bet you aren't one of them."

She narrowed her eyes at him. "What would make you presume anything about me?"

He lifted a broad shoulder. "Presumptions are a part of life. You made some about me—that I was not the type of man who would need to join strangers for Christmas—and I have made some about you."

"Do tell," she said, though in truth she was bracing herself. She was not sure she wanted him to tell at all.

"There's a look about you. A country girl."

A country girl? She had lived in the city now for nearly five years. She considered herself fairly sophisticated.

Not that you would know it at the moment. She was dressed in a pink parka and her jeans were stuffed into snow boots. On her hurried way out the back door, she had put her grand-pa's toque back on. Her cheeks were probably pink, and no doubt her nose was, too.

"Not a touch of makeup. Wholesome," he went on, ignoring the fact that she was looking daggers at him. "Giving. Christmas magic and all that. Hopelessly naive. Probably made a bad choice in a man and Grandpa has stepped in to find you a suitable partner. Right at Christmas. Cue the music."

He began to hum "White Christmas."

She hoped it wouldn't get stuck in her head.

"Are you always so insufferable?" she asked.

"I try...and that's out of character. Not giving at all. Tut-tut."

"Let me tell you my presumptions. You hate Christmas. I can tell by your obnoxious tone." She thought of adding, *No wonder you haven't been able to succeed at giving your daughter a good one*, but stopped herself. It would just be mean. And he was, unfortunately, right about the wholesome and giving part of her nature.

"I wondered about an ulterior motive in getting us here," Aidan said. "Who just invites strangers for Christmas?"

"Well, you can just quit wondering. You will never—never—meet a man with more integrity than my grandfather. He's invited strangers for

Christmas because he feels he has something to give, not to take anything."

"Humph," he said with an insulting lack of conviction.

Was Aidan Phillips annoying her on purpose? Surely her face had softened in sympathy at his vulnerable dad side, as he had revealed each of his Christmas failures? Now, he was successfully erasing that. If he was now trying to make her angry—a defense against her unwanted sympathy—it was working all too well!

"My grandfather might be trying to look after me. I hope not, but he's old and his heart is in the right place, which I'm sure you figured out when you accepted his generous invitation to spend Christmas at his home. I may be single, but really, you would both be presuming too much by thinking I would be interested in you!"

Of course, there was the momentary lapse over his hair, but he never had to know.

He stopped. It forced her to stop, too. She tilted her chin and glared at him.

"And you wouldn't be?" he asked, incredulous.

"Oh!" She fought a desire to take off her grandfather's toque and stuff it in her pocket so she wouldn't look quite so *folksy*. "Why would you sound so surprised? Do you have women flinging themselves at you all the time?"

"Yes." He cocked his head at her.

"I am not some country bumpkin who is going to be bowled over by your charm, Mr. Phillips," she said tightly.

"I don't have any charm."

"Agreed."

"You've had a heartbreak, just as I guessed."

The utter audacity of the man. It made her want to pick up a handful of snow and throw it in his face.

"There might be other reasons a woman would not fling herself at you," she suggested tightly. *Even though that one happened to be true.*

"There might be," he said skeptically.

*But, also true, perhaps a woman would recognize instantly that she was not in the same league as you*, she thought to herself. *Perhaps she'd recognize she had failed to hang on to a relationship with even a very ordinary guy, so what were her chances of—*

She stopped her train of thought because he was still watching her way too closely and she did not like the uneasy feeling she had that Aidan Phillips, astute businessman, could read her mind.

"It would be very old-fashioned to think a woman's main purpose in life is to find herself a mate," she told him primly.

"And yet here we are at an Old-Fashioned Country Christmas." He tilted his head at her, his eyes narrow and intent again. "Recent?"

"What?"

"The heartbreak?"

"I'm beginning to take a dislike to you."

"It's not my fault."

"That I dislike you?"

"That women fling themselves!"

"You're handsome and you're wealthy and you're extremely successful and perhaps somewhat intelligent, though it's a bit early to tell."

"I used rhotacism in a sentence!"

She ignored him. "Women fling themselves at you. You've become accustomed to it. They probably find the fact that you are a single dad bumbling through Christmas very endearing. Oh, boo-hoo, Mr. Phillips."

It occurred to her that her sarcasm might be coming more from a deep well of resentment that Mitchell was, at this very moment, surrounding himself with bikinis on a beach in Thailand than at Aidan Phillips, but she would take all the protection the shield of sarcasm could give her. Aidan was exactly the kind of man a woman needed to protect herself from. And worse, he knew it.

"Bumbling through Christmas?" he sputtered. "You call Christmas at the Happiest Place on Earth and at Santa's original place of residence bumbling?"

"Failures by your own admission," she said, with a toss of her head, "and should you have doubt, ask your daughter."

Aidan glared at her, though when he spoke, his voice was carefully controlled, milder than his glare. "I think I'm beginning to take a dislike to you, too."

"Good!"

"Good," he agreed. He continued, his voice softly sarcastic, "It's setting up to be a very nice quiet Christmas in the country, after all."

"Emphasis on quiet, since I won't be speaking to you."

"Starting anytime soon?" he asked silkily.

"Right now!"

"Good," he said again.

She couldn't resist. "Good," she said with a curt nod. They strode along the path back to the house in a silence that bristled.

She watched out of the corner of her eye as he yanked his cell phone from his pocket and began scrolling furiously, walking at the same time. It took him a few seconds to realize it wasn't going to work. He stopped.

"Is there cell service?" he asked tightly.

"We're not speaking."

"That's childish."

"You didn't seem to think so a few minutes ago."

"It's just a yes or no," he said.

"No." She should not have felt nearly as gleeful about the look on his face as she did. Clearly the thought of not being joined to his world, where he was in control of everything and everybody—with the possible exception of his daughter—was causing him instant discomfort.

"Will there be cell service at the house?"

"No."

"I'm expecting an important email. I have several calls I have to make."

"Did you get cell service in the Finnish Lapland?"

"Actually, they take pride in their excellent cell service all across Finland."

He managed to make that sound as if they had managed to be more *bumpkin* here than in one of the most remote places in the world.

Noelle had the sudden thought Tess's string of Christmas disappointments might, at a level she would not yet be able to articulate—despite being five going on twenty-one—have had a lot more to do with her father's ability to be absent while he was with her than the inadequacies of Disneyland or the Northern Lights.

"You can make the calls from his landline in the house," she said, maybe more sharply than she intended. "And I guess you could go to the library in the village and check emails. That's what my grandfather does. Mind you, he has to drive. You could take your helicopter. You could be there in minutes. Maybe even seconds! But it would cause a sensation. There would probably be that unwanted publicity involved."

"You're pulling my leg, aren't you?" He sounded hopeful. He was holding his phone out at arm's length, squinting at it, willing service to appear.

"Do I look like the type of person who would pull your leg?"

He regarded her suspiciously, but didn't answer.

It was because he didn't answer that she decided not to tell him there were a few "sweet spots" on the ranch. One was in the hayloft of the barn. You could get the magic bars on your cell phone to light up to two, and sometimes even three precious bars, if you opened the loft door and held your arm out. If the stars were aligned properly and the wind wasn't blowing. You had to lean out dangerously to take advantage of the service. It was a desperate measure to go sit out there in the cold trying to reconnect with the world.

And somehow she knew she'd be out there later tonight, looking at Mitchell's latest posts about his new and exciting life, tormenting herself with all that she wasn't.

She glanced at Aidan. When he felt her eyes on him, he shoved his cell phone in his pocket. His face was set in deep lines of annoyance, as if she had personally arranged the lack of cell service to inconvenience him.

They came over that rise in the road where they could see the house. She wondered if, in his eyes, it looked old and faintly dilapidated instead of homey and charming, especially with the snow, mounded up like whipped cream, around it. He did not even comment on the house at all, or on the breathtaking spectacle of sweeping landscapes and endless blue skies and majestic mountains.

Noelle thought that what she had said earlier in a pique might be coming true.

She disliked Aidan Phillips. A lot.

And that was so much safer than the alternative! She marched on ahead of him, without bothering to see if he followed.

# CHAPTER FOUR

AIDAN PHILLIPS WATCHED his hostess move firmly into the lead, her pert nose in the air and her shoulders set with tension.

He'd managed, and very well, too, to annoy her.

That could only be a good thing! He had no idea if the grandfather had ulterior motives in the matchmaking department. And despite Noelle's vehement denial, women did find him irresistible, exactly for one of the reasons she'd stated.

It was the single-dad thing that set women to cooing and setting out to rescue him. It had been most unwise on his part to share his Christmas catastrophes with someone he didn't even know. But there had been something in the wide set of her eyes, in the green depths of them, that had momentarily weakened him, made him want to unburden. But he'd known as soon as he had, by the sudden softness in her face and the that-poor-guy look that he'd come to so heartily re-sent, that weakness had been—as weakness inevitably was—a terrible mistake.

She'd even articulated his parenting journey. *Bumbling*.

To the best of his abilities, Aidan *was* bumbling through the challenges of being a single parent to a small girl who had lost her mother. It stunned him that his performance would be average at best, or even below average, he suspected, if there was a test available to rate these things.

The truth was, Aidan Phillips was used to being very, very good at things. He had the Midas touch when it came to money, and he had a business acumen that came to him as naturally as breathing. He was considered one of Canada's top business leaders, one to watch. His success was the envy of his colleagues and business competitors. At some instinctive level, he *knew* what to do. He knew when to expand and when to contract, whom to hire, where to experiment. He knew when to be bold. And when to fold.

He'd been called an overachiever most of his life and he considered it the highest form of a compliment.

But then, there was *the secret*.

He sucked at the *R*-word, as in *Relationships*. His marriage, which he had gone into with incredible confidence and high hopes, had been evidence of that. He'd been like an explorer dumped in a foreign land without a map. And instead of finding his way, he had become more and more lost…

His failure in this department made him insecure about his parenting, about his ability to relate to the more sensitive gender of the species, even a pint-size model like Tess.

He could not seem to get the equation right. His business mind needed an equation, but Tess resisted being a solvable puzzle. He loved his daughter beyond reason. From the first moment he'd held her tiny squirming body in his hands, he had been smitten…and yet there was a pervasive feeling of failing, somehow.

If he was looking for a success—and he was—it was Nana. She had come from an agency that specialized in these things, and to him she was like Mary Poppins, albeit without the whimsy.

She loved his daughter—and him—in her own stern way, and she knew things about children, in the very same way he knew them about business. She knew how to pull uncooperative hair into tight ponytails without creating hysteria. She knew the right bedtime stories, and read them without missing lines as he sometimes did, hoping to get off easy and early to make that important phone call. She knew about playdates with other little creatures who cried too easily, pouted, wanted to play princess and paint their fingernails and generally terrified the hell out of Aidan.

He was guiltily aware Nana's steadying presence allowed him to do what he was best at—work—with less guilt.

And so, Aidan was well aware he was *bumbling* through, doing his best and falling short, winning the unwanted pity and devotion of almost every woman who saw him with his daughter.

It's like they all somehow knew his secret failing, including this one marching ahead of him with her nose in the air.

The truth was, he'd had his reservations about the Old-Fashioned Country Christmas. And so had Nana. For once, he had overruled her, wanting something so desperately and not knowing how to get there.

Wanting his daughter to experience something he'd never had, not even when he had shared the Christmas season with his wife. He wanted her to have that joyous Christmas that was depicted in every carol and every story and every TV show and every movie.

Crazy to still believe in such things.

But the unexpected McGregor granddaughter did. Somehow, he knew Noelle believed. In goodness. And probably miracles. The magic of Christmas and all that rot. He hated it, and was drawn to it at the very same time.

Oh, boy. She was the kind of see-through-to-your-soul person that a guy like him—who had given up on his soul a long, long time ago—really needed to watch himself around.

If there was a palpable tension between Aidan and herself, Noelle noted things were not going much better in the house.

She dispensed with the toque immediately—she could not help feeling it contributed to the country bumpkin look—but her hair was flyaway and hissing with static underneath it. Aidan looked entertained by her efforts to pat it down, so she stopped, stomped the snow off her feet and left him in the porch.

Nana and her grandfather were having a standoff in the kitchen.

"Surely you don't think these filthy *things* belong on the counter?"

"Don't touch those. There are not filthy, they're greasy. There's a difference. They're engine parts. They're in order!"

"They don't belong in the kitchen!"

"It's my kitchen!"

"But I won't eat food that's been prepared on that." She waved a hand at the mess.

"It looks as if you could stand to miss a few meals."

"Oh! I never!"

"That's obvious, you dried-up old—"

"Grandpa."

In the back of her mind Noelle was thinking, *food.* Had her grandfather laid in enough food for guests? Had he planned for three meals a day for at least five people, plus snacks that would interest a five-year-old? And what about the rooms? Had he freshened them up? Laundered sheets and put out good towels? Most of the rooms in this large house had not been used in years.

The logistics of it, not to mention the squabbling, were beginning to give Noelle an awful headache, which worsened when Aidan came into the kitchen.

Underneath his jacket, he had on an expensive shirt, pure white and possibly silk, not the kind of shirt you generally saw on the ranch. He exuded a presence of good grooming and good taste and subtle wealth that made the room seem too small and somewhat shabby.

This whole idea was so ill conceived, Noelle decided desperately. Couldn't she just announce the Old-Fashioned Country Christmas was a terrible mistake and send them all home? At the moment it seemed everyone, including her grandfather, the instigator, would be more than pleased by such a turn of events!

"She told Tess the stove was dangerous," her grandpa reported furiously. "You know how many kids we've had through this house without a single burn victim?"

Yes, everyone would be more than pleased if an old-fashioned Christmas was canceled, except for Tess. Noelle's eyes were drawn to her stillness.

The little girl, in her candy-floss-pink outfit, with her gorgeous curls and pixie features, was standing off to the side, frozen as a statue, her hand resting on Smiley's head, her wide eyes going back and forth between her Nana and Noelle's grandfather.

"That's quite enough," Noelle said quietly, making a small gesture toward Tess.

All the adults in the room looked at the little girl.

Noelle remembered the orphaned child she had been, and she reminded her grandfather of that with a glance and a loudly cleared throat.

"Sorry," he mumbled in the direction of Nana. "I've become set in my ways."

Nana could have leaped at the opportunity to

agree, but in a reasonable tone she said, "I'd be happy to clean up the counters."

"I'll help," Noelle said quickly.

Her grandfather nodded. "But don't touch my engine parts. They're lined up in order. I'll put them away myself. You want to help me put up the outdoor Christmas lights this afternoon?" he asked Aidan, shooting a resentful look at Nana, as if she was displacing him from a house he now couldn't wait to get out of.

"Delighted," Aidan said, his tone cool and not delighted in the least.

Tess broke from her stillness. The tiny worried knot in her brow evaporated. She clapped her hands together. "We're just like a family," she declared.

"Isn't that the truth?" Aidan said pleasantly. Noelle shot him a look. She was almost certain his experiences with family—and with Christmas—had not been good ones. Maybe even before a horrible fire had changed everything?

Could she overcome her initial defensive reaction to him—to his hostility and his dislike of Christmas and his horrible cynicism—and change that?

Really, wasn't that what Christmas was all about? To think about others? Weren't the most meaningful gifts the ones you bestowed upon the strangers that came to your door? Wasn't that in keeping with the spirit of the first Christmas, when the wise men had followed the star to a manger?

Hadn't she been the recipient of amazing gifts from strangers and from family, when, at twelve, she had found herself facing her first Christmas as an orphan?

That was what she had to remember. It wasn't about her. It was about giving back what had been so freely given. All of them here were going to have to unite in a common goal.

To give motherless Tess—and maybe her daddy, too—a Christmas that would ease some of their painful memories. A Christmas that would be filled with a kind of magic that he had searched for and found all his money could not buy. A Christmas that would be overflowing with the true spirit of the day and the season.

Hopefully, it would make her grandfather's first Christmas without his partner of some fifty-odd years somewhat more bearable, too.

Since these were such happy thoughts, altruistic even, why did Noelle feel as if she was preparing to go into battle?

"Have you ever cut down your own Christmas tree before?" she asked Tess.

The little girl's eyes went very round. She clapped her hands together. A smile lit her face.

"No," she breathed. "We didn't have our own Christmas tree last year. Or the ugly Santa year."

Noelle noticed she had outgrown her rhotacism. Or a therapist had been hired.

Of course they wouldn't have had a tree of their own. Not in a glass igloo and not in the best hotel room money could buy.

Tess frowned with fierce concentration. "Did we before that, Daddy?"

"Of course, we did."

Noelle glanced at Aidan. His face was pained. Obviously, they had had their own Christmas tree once, a memory he was trying to outrun, whether he knew it or not.

"We'll go out and find a Christmas tree," Noelle promised her. "We won't stop looking until we find one that is absolutely right."

"A really big one?" Tess asked.

"Maybe. Or maybe it will be a really small one. We'll know when we see it. It's as if it will whisper to us, *I'm the one*."

"Really?" Tess asked.

"Really."

"Really?" Aidan said drily.

"I told you it was going to be perfect, Daddy," Tess whispered.

"It sounds dangerous," Nana said.

Grandpa rolled his eyes.

But it was Aidan's face that captivated Noelle.

He was, it seemed, trying to contain his cynicism as he looked at his little girl, his handsome face softened with hopefulness.

Despite all his skepticism and suspicion, he just wanted his little girl to be happy.

How hard could it be to put any animosity he had coaxed to the surface aside and make his Christmas wish come true?

Noelle took a deep breath. She knew what would make that little girl happy. The presence of her father. The absolute presence of him, without his emails and his phone calls and all the distractions that he had used to keep from doing the very thing his little girl needed him to do.

*Feeling.*

Noelle realized she wanted to engineer activities so that Tess spent as much time as possible with her daddy.

"Grandpa, maybe you and Nana could put up the lights this afternoon, after lunch. Aidan and Tess and I will go in search of the perfect tree."

Her grandpa looked as if he intended to protest. Strenuously. As did Nana. Aidan looked none too thrilled, either. He patted his shirt pocket, looking for the reassurance of the cell phone that wasn't there. Her grandfather's mouth opened. Nana lifted her hand as if in class, waiting for permission to register her complaint.

But Tess nearly melted. "Doesn't that sound purr-fect, Daddy?"

Nana's hand drifted down. Grandpa's mouth snapped shut. Aidan gave up his search for his cell phone, squatted in front of his child and let her wrap her arms around his neck.

"It does," he whispered, standing with her in his arms.

Looking at the two of them, an island of desperate need, Noelle felt the enormity of the responsibility she had just shouldered.

She turned her attention away. "Grandpa? Is there, um, a plan for lunch?"

Rufus looked inordinately pleased by the question. "Yes, indeed there is," he said. He pulled a rumpled piece of paper from his pocket. "Today for lunch is pizza!"

"You have that written down?" Noelle asked, astounded.

"For every day," he said. "Finishing with turkey and all the fixin's on Christmas."

He had a meal plan! For heaven's sake, maybe he had given this thing a great deal more thought than Noelle had given him credit for. Maybe her concerns about his mental wellness had been a bit overblown. On the other hand, he'd obviously been in the planning stages for a long time. Why hadn't he shared it with her? She intended to ask him that at the first opportunity!

"I love pizza," Tess said.

"I figured you would," Rufus said, smiling.

Still, even though he hadn't shared his idea with her, Noelle had to admit that maybe, just maybe, Rufus had the right idea, after all. Maybe Christmas should bring strangers together.

"It seems we're a long way from the nearest pizzeria," Aidan said with a certain skepticism.

Then again, maybe not.

Rufus retrieved several frozen pizzas from his chest freezer. While he scooped up engine parts and spirited them away to a new location, Noelle and Nana cleaned behind him. As Noelle watched out of the corner of her eye, Aidan and Tess carefully read the pizza boxes and prepared the pizzas for the oven.

By the time lunch was over, some of the tensions had faded. Immediately following lunch, Rufus directed everyone to their rooms. Noelle had, as surreptitiously as possible, inspected them. Again, her grandfather was prepared.

The rooms were dusted. The linens were clean. The upstairs bathroom was spotless. He'd definitely been preparing for this event for some time.

Probably he had started just about the time that Noelle had started to hear the change in his voice, from defeat to cautious enthusiasm for the season.

Why the secrecy? Why had he not included her in his planning?

Still, despite being a bit hurt by that, there was beginning to be a number of reasons for her to embrace this Christmas plan.

An hour later, she and Aidan had bundled Tess up and headed outside. Tess and Smiley raced ahead of them through the snow, Tess's laughter gurgling out of her as the old dog kept accidentally bumping her legs. Aidan did not look at home carrying an ax, but he had looked offended when Noelle had said she would carry it, along with the saw.

On a high piece of ground, before they entered a grove of trees, he stopped and checked his cell phone.

"Don't even bother," Noelle told him.

He squinted at her, as if realizing for the first time she was there. He put his cell phone away.

"So," Aidan asked, his voice threaded through with cynicism, "why the new plan? You and me looking for a Christmas tree, instead of me putting up lights with your grandfather?"

The nice feeling of this being a good idea that might work out after all shimmered like a mirage about to disappear.

Could he seriously not see how important it was for him to spend quality time with his daughter? Could he not see that it was a gift that he couldn't get cell service?

Still, didn't he have to figure that out for himself?

"You're onto me, Mr. Phillips," she said, blinking at him and smiling sweetly. "Despite me telling you I'm definitely not interested in you, you have seen right through the charade, because what woman couldn't be interested in you, really? So I have engineered this opportunity to spend time with you. I am hoping in the wholesome activity of cutting down a Christmas tree you will see I am excellent with both dogs and children. You will see I am both playful and intelligent, practical and an excellent problem-solver."

His lips were twitching reluctantly. "All that in the cutting down of a tree?"

"It's not simply cutting down a tree. Selection of the tree is important."

"Oh, yes," he said cynically, though his eyes were still sparking with laughter, "the tree is going to speak to us, if I recall."

"That's right. So add 'intuitive' to my checklist as a great mate. Cutting it down and getting it home might be more complicated than you thought. You'll see my strengths. Naturally," she said demurely, "I'll be judging yours, as well. Strength, in particular, is important to a

CARA COLTER

woman searching for a life mate. Possibly more so than intelligence."

"This is the second time you've brought my intelligence up for debate."

"Really? I'll put it in the plus column. That you can count."

"I hardly know what to say."

"Yes, well, that goes in the minus column then. A certain social ineptitude."

He actually laughed. He was trying hard not to, but he did.

His laughter was rich and genuine, and it made him quite extraordinarily handsome. Tess ran back to him, delighted by the sound, wanting to be part of it. Did he really laugh so seldom that it drew his daughter's attention to him?

"What, Daddy, what?" she insisted, tugging on his sleeve.

"Our new friend, Noelle, is very entertaining."

"What does that mean?" Tess asked.

"Playful and intelligent," Noelle supplied helpfully. Was it a weakness to want to make him laugh again and again? And not just for Tess's benefit?

He set down the ax, bent down, scooped up a handful of snow and tossed it at Noelle. It happened so swiftly she didn't have time to get her hands up. The snow hit her toque and drifted down her face.

"I hope," Noelle sputtered, "you didn't consider that a snowball? Definitely in the minus column for you."

She bent, put down the saw, scooped up her own handful of snow and expertly rounded it in her hands, compacting it, firming it up. She inspected it, the perfect ball, hefted it experimentally from hand to hand.

"Wait a minute," he said, holding up his hands, mock surrender.

She pulled her arm back. He gave a shout and raced away from her. The snowball exploded in the middle of his back.

Tess shrieked with laughter. The dog barked.

"Show me how!" Tess insisted.

"Hey, no fair," he yelled. "Two against one."

*"Au contraire,"* Noelle called after him. "All is fair in, well, you know."

She armed Tess with a snowball. Tess chased after her father, who ran away but slowed down enough for her to get him. The little girl was laughing so hard she could barely launch the snowball, let alone land the target. But she had the idea now. She knelt in the snow, giggling fiendishly as she shaped her next snowball.

And while Aidan watched his daughter, amused, Noelle crept forward into range and let loose the four snowballs she had made and cradled in the crook of her arm.

Wham, wham, wham, wham, in quick succession.

"Where on earth did you learn to aim like that?"

"I'm a country girl," she reminded him. "You don't want to let me too near a rifle if you thought that was good."

"Noted," he said. And then he was leaning down, picking up snow, shaping a perfect hard ball between his own gloved hands.

Tess shot forward with her snowball and gave him a good hard shot in the knees.

"Ouch," he yelled with fake pain, while his daughter howled with glee. He came after Noelle.

In minutes the air was filled with laughter, shrieking, the dog barking and snowballs.

Half an hour later, they all lay side by side in the snow, soaked and exhausted from both laughing and playing so hard.

"Did I win, Daddy, did I win the snowball fight?"

"Oh, yeah, not a doubt there."

Aidan turned his head. Noelle could feel him looking at her.

"Off the charts in the playful department," he said. He got to his feet and hovered over her. He held out a gloved hand, and after just a second's hesitation, she took it.

"Oh, well," she said. "When you're not beautiful, you have to make up for it in other ways."

The laughter left his face. He scowled and drew her to her feet, his strength easy. She was standing way too close to him. His scent was heady and crisp. She should have stepped away. He should have let go.

But she did not step away, and he did not let go.

"Not beautiful?" he asked gruffly and then even more strongly. "Not beautiful? What?"

# CHAPTER FIVE

NOELLE WAS BEING lifted up by what she saw in Aidan's eyes, lifted up out of her body and delivered to a place where angels gathered.

That place was dangerous, she told herself.

And yet, still, even knowing the danger, it was hard to break the bond between them, between their hands, and their eyes, their bodies so close together, radiating warmth from all their exertions. Even their breath was frosty and tangled, as if they were breathing in the essence of each other.

Noelle yanked her snow-soaked mittens out of his, but somehow she didn't move. Couldn't. He was drinking in her face with a look she could not move away from.

As if he was thirsty and she was a long, cool drink of water. Or maybe she was the thirst and he was the drink of water.

"Not beautiful," she stammered. "I'm not."

"What would make you believe such a thing?"

Her mouth moved to begin reiterating a long list of proofs, but not a single sound came out.

"I knew it," he growled with a fearsome anger. "Some dog in your past—possibly your recent past—has made you believe this thing."

She could still say nothing, stunned by what she saw in his eyes.

He wasn't saying this to make her feel good. It wasn't some pat line. It came from the deepest part of him, a place where there were no lies or deceptions, only truth.

And if she doubted, Aidan took off his glove. He reached out with a gentleness that almost made her cry for the affirmation of his truth in it. His hand warm, his skin silk over iron, touched her cheek, scraped it, rested there. She could not move away from his touch, captive to his unexpected tenderness.

"You are so beautiful," he said softly. "You may be the most beautiful woman I have ever seen."

Her mouth fell open. She could feel herself leaning toward whatever she saw in his eyes.

"Daddy, are you going to kiss Noelle?"

The little voice, inquisitive, delighted, yanked them apart.

His hand fell down. He shoved it in his pocket. "Of course not!" he said.

"No!" Noelle agreed.

He spun away from her. "I have no idea where that ax is."

She scanned the churned-up snow. "When you find it, the saw should be nearby."

And then some nervous tension broke between them, and the three of them were laughing all over again, kicking up snow until they found the ax and saw.

Back on their journey, after the detour, they entered another grove of trees.

"This is mostly balsam fir," Noelle said. She took a deep breath. "Can you smell them? I think they're the best Christmas trees. They're native to my grandfather's land."

"I can smell them!" Tess said.

They wandered through them, judging this one and that, Tess leaning close to several to smell them and to see if they whispered.

"You might want to explain to her the whispering part is not exactly literal."

"Ah, ye of little faith," Noelle said. "When did you stop believing in magic?"

He didn't answer that, just looked away quickly so that she knew it had been a long, long time ago.

Suddenly Tess, who had been flitting from tree to tree like a bumble bee pollinating flowers, stopped. She stood in front of a tree. She cocked her head. She was utterly still.

And then she turned and looked at them, her face incredulous.

"It whispered!" she said.

Aidan took a surprised step back and looked at Noelle. "Exactly what kind of enchantress are you?" he said.

"Apparently the beautiful kind," she said, laughing.

"But that's the most dangerous kind of all," he said softly, and suddenly that near-miss, near-kiss moment was sizzling in the air between them.

Imagine a man like Aidan Phillips thinking she was dangerous.

Still, she could not linger in the power of that.

"You don't know the meaning of the word *dangerous*," she said. "But chopping down a tree could change that."

"I think there are all kinds of danger, and sometimes the more subtle kinds are way more threatening than the sharp blade of a big ax."

"Is it perfect?" Tess asked. "Is it?"

They all stood looking at the tree. It was about five feet tall, and mounded with snow. Aidan stepped forward and shook it. The snow slid off it and down his back.

"Just taking one for the team," he said. "No need for concern."

The tree, without snow, was nicely filled out on one side and not so much on the other.

Though it looked big from Tess's viewpoint, it was obviously very small, maybe a little taller than Noelle was. The branches were too far apart in places. There was another place where a large branch had been damaged and all the needles had turned brown. The top had taken off crazily in a different direction than the bottom, giving the tree quite a crooked lean.

It was, without a doubt, the most perfect Christmas tree any of them had ever seen.

"I'm going to try to break this to you gently," Noelle told Aidan an hour later, "but you are no woodsman."

He had, by now, stripped off his jacket. And his mittens. The sweat was beaded on his brow.

Really? She could have offered to go back to the barn and retrieve the chainsaw. But that would have taken all the fun out of it.

Fun and something else. There was something gloriously breathtaking about seeing the male animal pit his strength against the elements.

Plus, ever since the near kiss, Noelle's senses felt heightened. The light, especially the way it threaded through his coal-dark hair, seemed exquisite. The sharp smell of the tree had intensified as his ax bit into bark and pulp and, finally, sap. Tess's laughter, as she made angels and covered the dog with snow and wrote her name with footprints, filled the glade with fairy music.

Noelle's *you-are-no-woodsman* taunt earned her a good-natured glare, and Aidan renewed his efforts to chop through the trunk of the tree. Finally, it was still upright, but only by the merest of threads of broken wood fiber.

"Move the women, children and dogs to safe ground," he shouted. "Timber."

The tree didn't so much fall, as kind of gently slide down, with a whisper rather than a crash. Several of its branches cracked, making the tree even less perfect than it had been before.

"That was somewhat anticlimactic," Aidan declared, breathing hard.

But Tess was beside herself with excitement. After resting briefly, all of them, ignoring the discomfort of prickly needles and sharp little branches, grabbed on to the tree and began to drag it through the snow.

Night came early at this time of year, and it was nearly dark by the time they got the tree almost back to the house. They were breathless and tired and utterly happy.

They paused for a rest as the house came into view. It was drenched in the dying light of the day, in soft pinks and muted golds and fiery oranges. As the darkness deepened around it, an owl hooted, and in the far distance, a pack of wolves began to sing a haunting and wild song.

"Wolves?" Aidan asked, surprised.

"Yes, relative newcomers to this area."

"Are they on the other side of that field?" he asked.

Noelle smiled at the fierce, protective note in his voice. "The sound really carries on nights like this. I don't think they're close, at all. And that's not a field, though I can see why you would think so when it's covered with snow like that. It's a pond. My grandfather always clears it Christmas Day for skating."

"Oh, too bad, we didn't bring skates. Tess doesn't have any yet. I haven't skated for years. And Nana? Can you imagine?"

They shared a laugh.

A light turned on in the house, throwing a golden glow out the window and lighting up a pathway through the snow. It beckoned them, calling them home, to the promise of warmth against the cooling of the day, a promise of safety against the mysteries of the woods in the night.

And then a door slapped open.

"Are you done yet?" Nana's shrill voice carried across the snow as clearly as the wolf song had.

"Art takes time!" Rufus yelled back. "Where have you been? I needed you to hand me the string of lights marked number fourteen. I had to get down and get it myself. I'm old. I can't be expected to go up and down a ladder a hundred times!"

It was possibly the first time Noelle had ever heard her grandfather refer to himself as old.

"Oh, be quiet, you ancient coot. Do you ever stop complaining? I was helping! I went in to find something for supper."

"Do you think this has been going on since we left?" Aidan asked. He didn't even try to hide his amusement.

"No doubt. I'm not sure what it is. My grandfather never acts the way he does with her."

"You don't know what it is?" Aidan said, looking at her with interest. A smile was tickling his lips.

"No. Do you?"

"It's the age-old game."

She felt shocked. "But my grandmother has only been gone a few months. It wouldn't be right."

"Maybe that's what he thinks, too," Aidan offered softly. "That it needs to be fought. That it isn't right."

"They don't like each other," she insisted, but for some reason she was thinking she had said nearly those same words to Aidan. *I don't like you.*

And he had said them to her.

And then, despite that initial animosity, only hours later, they had come very close to kissing. A shiver went up and down her spine as she contemplated the fact that she might be playing the age-old game with Aidan.

It had to stop. It could only end in pain.

Her grandfather's voice came with clarity through the cold air and across the snow again.

"I hope you didn't meddle with supper."

"It's already in the oven."

"I have a plan I'm following!"

"Oh, well," Nana said, unrepentant. "I think I can figure out how to heat a frozen lasagna."

"That's not for tonight! Tonight was cabbage rolls. It was marked right on the containers. I had Mrs. Bentley mark them."

Noelle smiled. Her grandfather was so organized he'd had one of the neighbors prepare frozen dinners for him and for the company he was expecting. It was just so endearing...and yet again, it nagged at her. Much preparation had gone into this. Why hadn't he told her what he was up to?

Apparently Nana missed the endearing part of an old widower hosting guests for Christmas.

"Oh, don't be so stuck in your ways. The label must have fallen off. Aidan and Tess and Noelle will be home soon, and they'll be hungry.

Shouldn't they be home by now? What if Aidan's bleeding to death out there?"

"Maybe all of them got attacked by that wolf pack. Being eaten as we speak."

"What wolf pack?"

"You can't hear them? If you'd stop talking for three seconds… Plug in the lights."

"Wolves?" That shrill note again.

"Plug in the damned lights!"

And into the sudden silence and the gathering darkness, the lights of the house winked on. They were bright primary colors: red and yellow, blue and green. They ran around the roofline, making globes of reflected color in the snow. They marked the gables. They wrapped around the porch pillars and the railings, and they outlined the windows. Noelle could not be sure how two old people had gotten this much done.

Maybe, despite the bickering, there was a certain magic in the air.

Certainly, the house seemed to be saying that. It had transformed from an old ranch house to a gingerbread house, something worthy of a fairy tale, in just an afternoon.

There was something about standing here, with Aidan and Tess, listening to the quarreling of Rufus and Nana in the distance, that made Noelle's heart stand still. And in the silence of her heart not beating, she was sure she heard a little voice.

There *are* other ways that game can end, it said: all good fairy tales end with *and they lived happily-ever-after.*

But Noelle reminded herself firmly of the red dress in her closet, her reminder of broken dreams. This was no fairy tale, she admonished herself sternly. There was no point casting Aidan in the role of a prince, despite his lapse in calling her beautiful and despite the near-miss kiss. He had made it abundantly clear he was not interested in a romance, and that she had better not be, either!

Grabbing the tree again, Noelle moved deliberately away from the lure of the magic in the air and toward the house. Aidan and Tess joined her and they dragged the tree up onto the porch. And then Noelle and Aidan stood, looking at it, while Tess danced around it.

Rufus and Nana admired their find and declared it perfect.

"Are we going to decorate it tonight?" Tess asked. "Please? Please? Please?"

There was something about the hopefulness of a child that made magic very hard to outrun.

# CHAPTER SIX

As IT TURNED out there was no tree-decorating that night. Despite a valiant effort to keep her eyes open, Tess went to sleep during dinner. She fell asleep instantly and completely, her hand clutched around her fork. She suddenly just sagged, the fork dropped, and she would have slid to the floor, like a silk dress off a stool, if her father had not risen from his own chair and scooped her up.

Aidan looked down into Tess's sleeping face, and Noelle felt it was a moment worthy of a painting. Not mother and child, but something even more precious, perhaps, for the rarity of its capture.

Father and child.

Strength and vulnerability. Independence and dependence. Largeness and tininess. Worldliness and innocence.

Aidan's face was a study in contrasts: the softness of love, but underneath that a certain fierce protectiveness that she had glimpsed when he'd heard the wolves. This child in his arms? This was what he was willing to die for.

And then he was gone from the dining room, and Noelle felt her own weariness catch up with her. It had been a jam-packed day, full of surprises, physical activity and emotional twists and turns. It had been sometimes exhilarating and sometimes exhausting.

"If you could leave the dishes," she said to Nana and her grandfather, "I'll look after them in the morning. Good night."

She sought the safety of her room. It was untouched by time. A bed was covered in the pillows, quilt and plush throw—all in shades of pink and white—that she had brought with her when she had moved here at age twelve.

Her grandmother had made the curtains, sheer fabric embossed with pink polka dots, and embellished them with frilly trim. Really, her adult eye could see it was too much, like the room was the unfortunate result of a mating between cotton candy and a tutu. Noelle's teen self was represented by photograph posters on the wall, one of a field of dandelions and one of a rainbow over an old barn. They told her to Dream Big and Never Give Up. The silver-framed picture of her mom and dad was on the dresser.

Except for the addition of the posters when she was around sixteen, Noelle did not change things. She had always loved the room just the way it was, even when she was old enough to want something else. To this day, she loved the remnants of her old life, the bedding she and her mother had chosen together.

The bed was a twin. When she and Mitchell had come to meet her grandparents she had stayed in this room, and he down the hall. Even though her grandparents knew she was living with Mitchell, they had not approved of the arrangement, and Noelle felt it would have been disrespectful to share a room with her boyfriend under her grandparents' roof.

Noelle felt glad of that now. That this room was what it had always been to her, untainted by unhappy memories, a haven in a world that had turned topsy-turvy on her more than once. She got her pajamas out of her suitcase, put them on and flipped out the light. It was usually very dark out here in the country, but tonight brightness from the Christmas lights reflecting off the snow on the roof came through her window and cast her room in muted rainbows. She crawled under her covers, appreciating again the freshly laundered linens, and all her grandfather's hard work to welcome her and others to his home.

She realized she hadn't talked to him as she had intended.

And then she realized she hadn't gone to the barn to check Mitchell's many social media posts for the day, either.

It wasn't too late. It was early. She could get up. She could hear her grandfather and Nana downstairs, the quiet clink of dishes being washed, their voices low and conversational, for once.

A good time to leave them alone and not a good time to find out why she, Noelle, had been excluded from his grand plan for an old-fashioned Christmas.

This would be the perfect time to slip out the door and sneak to the nearest place on the ranch that got cell service.

But her muscles ached pleasantly from chasing through the snow today and from hauling the tree home. She found herself unable to leave the sense of safety and security in her room, unwilling to get out from under her warm down quilt, not wanting to leave the state of languid relaxation both her mind and body were enjoying.

But then she heard sounds and realized Aidan must have tucked Tess into the little bed in the room under the eaves. Now he was in the hall bathroom, brushing his teeth. The water ran for a while longer. Possibly he was shaving. It all seemed very intimate!

Then his footsteps padded by Noelle's door as he went down the hall. She heard him go into the room next to hers, and through the thinness of the old walls she was sure she could hear his clothes coming off and whispering to the floor.

The springs of the bed next door creaked. It seemed to her that he had not had time to put something else on. What would he wear for pajamas? Did he wear pajamas? She had the sudden, totally uninvited thought that he might have slipped in between the sheets naked.

The fact that she would have such a thought made her blush. She wondered if these wayward images in her mind were going to make her blush the next time she saw him.

Her own pajamas now seemed woefully inadequate. She had chosen them for the ranch, for opening presents Christmas morning with her grandfather, not with Aidan Phillips! Red flannel, printed with penguins wearing Santa hats. Was she going to have to change every time she went down the hall to use the bathroom?

Why? To impress Aidan Phillips?

To make him whisper *beautiful* again?

It was all very awkward. It felt suddenly as if the sanctity of her room and her home had been invaded. As if a fine tension had crept into her snug nest. She had never felt this way when Mitchell was down the hall!

Red dress, she whispered to herself, her reminder of the pain of broken dreams, a reminder not to leave herself open to debilitating romantic fantasies.

*I'll never be able to sleep now,* she thought, watching the gentle play of the Christmas lights on her bedroom ceiling.

And it was the last thought she had before morning.

Aidan lay awake in the unfamiliar bed for a long time, contemplating the day. The room was humble, not what he was used to. A small bed was crowded under a sloped roof that looked as if it had leaked a long time ago. A spring was poking him in his behind. Cheery Christmas lights were shining in the small window, and it was irritating.

But the worst thing was that he, iron man of self-control, had nearly kissed a woman he barely knew. He had told her she was beautiful and watched as the sun rose in her eyes at the compliment, as if Noelle was not used to receiving them.

Aidan considered himself a smart man. And he knew what the smart thing to do would be. It would be to get up in the morning and announce something had come up, that they wouldn't be able to stay for Christmas, after all.

But then he thought of Tess's enjoyment of the day, her deep pleasure in small things: her kinship with the old dog, her glee in the snow, her wonder in finding the perfect tree, her happy exhaustion at the end of the day. He could not remember a day—ever—not even after full agendas in Disneyland, where she had not hauled out her collection of stories to be read as the day died. Tonight, the stories were not even unpacked.

Would he really shatter Tess's Christmas in order to protect himself? No, he wouldn't and he couldn't. But he had to be on guard.

"On guard," he muttered, very softly, so that his voice would not carry through the paper-thin walls. "On guard, on guard, on guard." The chant, unfortunately, seemed to be taking on the tune of "Frosty the Snowman," as if some unwanted magic was worming its way inside of him.

"You can do anything for a few days," Aidan told himself firmly. And he knew, with a touch of satisfaction, that it was true. He would make any sacrifice to allow his daughter happiness.

Maybe he wasn't such a colossal failure as a dad, after all.

Noelle awoke to familiar sounds: her grandfather opening the back door to bring wood in, the sounds of coffee beans being ground, the old iron door on the woodstove creaking open. She glanced at the bedside clock. It was very early.

She got up, and hesitated over the pajamas. It seemed too early to get dressed. It seemed like some kind of concession to *him* that she did not feel comfortable in her own home wearing what she had always worn. So, defiantly, she left them on. In her closet was an old plaid robe, and she put that over the pajamas. And then Noelle determinedly shoved her feet in the only slippers she had brought with her. The old ranch house floors could be like ice in the morning.

She looked down at her feet and warned herself to stop worrying about Aidan Phillips's impressions of her.

Her grandfather was kneeling in front of the stove, blowing lightly, coaxing heat from last night's embers, feeding in little pieces of kindling.

"You're up early," he said. "I'm glad. I got some things to show you."

He pulled a file down off the top of the fridge and presented it to her with shy pride. Noelle opened it.

"You can find so much stuff on the interstate," her grandfather said eagerly, hovering over her shoulder. "The library has a printer you can use for twenty-five cents a sheet."

From the thickness of the file, the library should be able to buy a new printer strictly from the proceeds of her grandfather's printing activities.

In the file were snow activities for children. Coloring snow with spray bottles of water and food coloring. Ice globes made with water frozen in balloons. Creative snowmen. And women. And snow caterpillars. Homemade snow globes. Feeders for birds. Frozen soap bubbles. "Noughts and Crosses" in the snow. Snow forts and snow castles.

"Wow," Noelle said, shutting the file.

"Which one should we do today? With Tess?"

"We could let her choose. I think the morning will probably be used up decorating the tree."

"I've got all the decorations in the attic ready to bring down."

"Grandpa." Noelle tapped the file. "You've been collecting ideas for quite some time."

He nodded happily.

"And you've done a lot of work planning meals. And getting rooms ready."

He seemed to figure out this was going somewhere. He moved over to the counter and his ancient coffee maker. He shot her a look out of the corner of his eye and busied himself measuring his freshly ground beans.

"Why didn't you tell me?" she asked softly.

"I'm your family. Why didn't you let me know? Why were you making Christmas plans without me?"

"Without you?" he said. "That's silly. I couldn't have Christmas without you!"

"That's not what I meant. I meant the ad on I-Sell. I meant telling me about Aidan and Tess and the Old-Fashioned Country Christmas. Why did you keep me in the dark?"

"It was a surprise," he said stubbornly.

"You know I don't really like surprises."

"Well, that's just it," he said, his back completely to her now as he fiddled with the coffee maker.

"What's just it?"

His shoulders hunched uncomfortably.

"Tell me."

At that moment an ear-splitting scream came from upstairs. "Stop, stop! You slathering beast!"

Noelle catapulted up the stairs. Her grandfather was already going up them two at a time.

At the top of the stairs, Aidan was coming out of his room. She nearly collided with him. Despite the fact that the screaming continued, she felt the world go still around her.

His hair was sleep-roughened. There was a shadow of morning whisker on his face.

And he was naked.

Partially naked.

He was wearing pajama bottoms, but his chest and torso were free of clothing. Deliciously so.

There was a carved beauty to his physique that was so compelling Noelle felt completely able to ignore the fact that it sounded as if Nana was being murdered in her bedroom.

His pajama bottoms were plaid, and hung very low on his hips. His feet were bare. How come she had never noticed how incredibly sexy bare feet were before?

"Get off me!" Nana shrieked.

"Oh, stop it," Rufus said. "It's just a dog."

It seemed to Noelle that Aidan's gaze might have rested on what showed of her penguin-pajamas-clad legs jutting out from under the housecoat for just a little too long. Her feet were not sexily bare. They were stuffed into slippers her grandmother and grandfather had given her a long time ago.

"Cookie Monster?" he said, as if he, too, was able to shut out the sounds of Nana screaming.

"Animal." She tilted her chin just to let him know she didn't care what he thought. Though a part of her did. Very much.

"Ah." He turned from her and went down the hallway.

In a daze, Noelle followed Aidan and they both stood in the doorway of Nana's bedroom.

Smiley had invaded. He was on her bed. He had her arms pinned under the covers, his huge paws straddling her, and he was feverishly licking thick gobs of cold cream off her face.

Rufus went and pulled the dog off, barely able to contain his gleeful snickering. Noelle couldn't help feeling he was doubly pleased because he had escaped answering her questions.

But then, terribly, Nana began to cry. "I was dreaming of wolves and—" She buried her poor face, cold cream rearranged unattractively, in her hands. Rufus's delight died on his face. He handed the dog off to Aidan, who looked stunned and uncomfortable, and turned back to Nana.

"There, there," he said, and went and sat on the edge of the bed. He pried a hand away from her face and patted it awkwardly. She turned and buried her face in his shirt. If the cold cream being slathered down the front of him bothered him, it didn't show. His hand slid to her hair.

"There, there," he said again. "You're fine. Everything's okay."

# CHAPTER SEVEN

Aidan backed out of the room hastily, dog firmly in his grasp He let go of the dog, and actually pulled the door shut behind him as if Nana and Rufus might need a little privacy! Smiley slunk away.

"Is she always…um, like this?" Noelle asked. The hallway felt very narrow. It felt as if his chest was nearly touching her.

She noticed his hair was a little messy. She had to stick her hands in her housecoat pockets to resist the urge to touch it, to smooth it into place.

*Red dress, red dress, red dress.*

"No," Aidan said, having no idea of the danger his hair was in, or the danger she found herself in. "Never. She's usually very stoic."

"Daddy!"

Another shrill distraction, thank heavens.

"Nice quiet morning at the ranch?" Aidan gave Noelle a wry grin that took the edge off the sarcasm and moved by her to fetch Tess. His naked chest passed within half an inch of her own penguin-pajama-clad one.

"What's wrong with Nana?" she heard Tess ask, and Noelle could hear the fear in her voice.

"She had a bad dream."

"Like I have sometimes?" The fear was already dissipating, her father's calm voice acting like sunshine on fog.

"Yes," he said. "Everything is okay."

He came back into the hallway, the little girl in his arms, nestled securely against the solidness of his chest. Her hair was even messier than his, and again Noelle had an urge to tame those tendrils with her fingertips.

It wasn't just him that had her danger signals blinking on high. It was both of them, this little girl so tugging at her heartstrings. Not as easy to defend against even with her red dress mantra!

"I like your pajamas," Tess told Noelle solemnly. "And your slippers."

"Thank you," Noelle said just as solemnly, and suddenly she was glad she had left on the pajamas and put on the slippers, after all.

"I'm hungry," Tess said, a little girl who had missed her dinner.

"What do you like for breakfast?" Noelle asked.

"Apple Bits." Tess named the popular children's cereal.

"Well, let's see what we have."

Sadly, Aidan put Tess down and went to get dressed.

Tess and Noelle went downstairs and put the dog—who was by the back door making noises like he might be sick—outside. Shockingly her grandfather had Apple Bits. Or maybe it wasn't so shocking. Since he was so organized, he'd probably sent out questionnaires asking what people liked for breakfast.

And so the day began.

Considering its rocky start—with her grandfather evading her questions and Nana being lovingly attacked by Smiley—everything turned good after that.

When Rufus came downstairs he was whistling. When Nana followed, twenty minutes or so later, she looked relaxed and almost happy.

"I'm making pancakes," Rufus announced.

"We've already had cereal," Noelle said.

He looked crushed until Nana said she'd love pancakes. She added that she loved a man who could cook a good breakfast, and Rufus practically preened as he got his blackened cast-iron pan down off its hook over the woodstove.

Noelle had to race onto the porch before she

let the laughter out. Aidan was right behind her. They laughed until their stomachs hurt.

And then with Tess "helping" they wrestled the tree in the door and into the stand, and stood back to admire it. Aidan put the lights on first, avoiding, just barely, words that should not be used around children.

When he was done, Rufus and Nana joined them and boxes of decorations were hauled from the attic. Rufus put on Christmas music and Aidan's groan seemed as if it were mostly for show. Tess was allowed to choose all the decorations. She was in charge of the bottom of the tree and the adults did the top. Smiley was let back in, and he curled up in his basket in the kitchen and refused to join them, though every now and then they would hear a giant wet burp from him that would send them into gales of laughter.

When the tree was done, Nana's objections—which seemed perfunctory, too—that hot chocolate would spoil lunch were quickly dismissed and they all sat in the living room admiring the tree and sipping the beverage.

Though they were near strangers, a sense of knowing each other—of family—was growing between them.

It was because Tess had brought them something they could not have had without her, the magic of making Christmas for a child.

"Oh!" Noelle suddenly remembered. "One last thing. The house isn't ready until the wreath goes on the door."

She got up and hunted through the decoration boxes until she found it. Old roping lariats had been carefully formed into a wreath shape, threaded through with a thick red ribbon that had once been bright but was now faded. Nestled in the curves of the rope and the ribbon were wooden letters—painted bright green by Noelle when she was very young, before her parents had died—that spelled out a single word: *HOPE*.

Aidan was eyeing her find with spectacular distaste, and she supposed it was old and ghastly and hokey. But she loved it. It felt like her grandmother was right here, as if all the love they'd shared was right here.

Noelle took it to the front door and went outside in her socks.

"You want some help?"

She saw Aidan had slipped out with her. "You don't look very impressed with my grandmother's wreath."

"Don't I?"

"No."

"I'm cynical, that's all. It's not the wreath, it's the word."

"Hope?"

"Aw, yes," he said. "What does it mean exactly?"

She gave him a quizzical look. "Isn't it obvious?"

"Tell me," he insisted.

"It's what Christmas is full of—hope. Hope for love. Hope for family. Hope for joy. Hope for a better world. Hope that hardships can be healed. Hope that someday we can think of the ones we have lost with peace instead of grief."

"That's a tall order," he said.

"Well, Christmas is known as a time you can hope for anything at all."

"Hope," he said softly. "Personally, I think that may be the most dangerous thing of all. Maybe it just sets up an expectation that can never be met."

"I'm not sure if that's cynical," Noelle said softly, "or just plain sad. No, I don't need your help. Thanks for offering. I'd rather do it myself."

"As you wish."

And he stepped back inside, leaving her to contemplate that. Who on earth thought hope was the most dangerous thing of all?

Someone who had been hurt very badly. He must have loved his wife very much. Noelle took her time hanging the wreath, and when she went in, lunch was ready.

To her grandfather's chagrin—he had planned soup and buns—Tess had asked for peanut butter and jam sandwiches. Then, when she only ate a quarter of one, Nana muttered about the hot chocolate spoiling lunch.

After lunch, Rufus hauled out his file of activities, but Nana sniffed and suggested gingerbread houses.

"I don't have the stuff to make that," Rufus protested, apparently not liking being thrown off his game plan for the second time in less than an hour.

"You think you're the only one who can have a good idea?" Nana asked, her tone combative. The truce was apparently over between them. "Out. Shoo… I'll get the gingerbread ready."

Grumbling, her grandfather said he had chores to do in the barn.

"Do you need help?" Aidan asked.

"What I need is some alone time!"

Only Noelle knew he was being so rude because he was trying to hide a pony!

"How about a snowman?" she said brightly.

"I think snow person is the current politically correct term," Aidan said.

The snow was all wrong. It was too cold and it made the snow dry and powdery. The snow person collapsed twice before Aidan came up with the idea of adding water to the snow. Even so, he was a terrible snowman: small and lop-sided, and his eyes kept falling out of his head.

Still, Tess loved him and declared him the most perfect snowman ever.

Rufus did not return for making the ginger-bread house, which might have been a good thing. Like the snowman, it was a less-than-stellar gingerbread house.

Gumdrops slid haphazardly down the side of it. One of the walls was collapsing under the weight of too much icing. A chunk broke off and Aidan ate it before they could repair it. Then they broke a chunk off for Tess to eat.

All in all, the house was quite ghastly, but Tess declared it the most perfect gingerbread house ever, so they were all happy.

Everyone seemed to have turned in early again tonight, except Noelle's grandfather, who went outdoors to do more chores.

"I'll come," Noelle said. Side by side they fed the horses, Gidget shoving the larger ones out of the way.

"Is the pony for Tess?" Noelle asked with trepidation.

"Yes. She hasn't seen her yet. Just keep her on the other side of the house for as long as you can."

"Her father said she couldn't have one, you know."

"Well, because he doesn't have a place to keep it. I do."

She sighed. That insinuated an ongoing relationship with the Phillipses. She was not sure her grandfather—or, for that matter, herself—should have hopes on that score. And hope was hard, after a day like today, with that growing sense of comfort and safety and family. How did you let that go when it was time?

Noelle was determined to finish the conversation that had started that morning.

"I need to know why you didn't tell me. A pony implies a great deal of before-thought."

"Humph, the pony was easier than trying to think how to feed a crowd for a couple of days. Your grandma looked after all that."

The longing had been in the background all day: as they put up the tree and decorated with her grandmother's collections of ornaments.

"She'd like the house full of people," he said.

"Though if she'd been here, you wouldn't have done it."

"True."

"Tell me why I was kept in the dark."

Her grandfather looked at her. "You don't like surprises. You don't even like changes. You would have tried to talk me out of it. Remember when I did tell you? I got a lecture about the dangers of the interstate."

"*Lecture* is overstating it!"

"The longer you knew about it, the longer you would have worked on me. Maybe you would have even tried to put a stop to it behind my back. For my own good."

Noelle desperately wanted to deny this, but she couldn't.

"You would have said no to the pony, you would have said people weren't really going to come, and that I was being tricked and cheated."

"That makes me sound like an awful wet blanket, but I would have just been trying to protect you, Grandpa."

"I know. But, Ellie, I'm a grown man. It's a bit insulting that you think you have to protect me."

She was silent, surprised by this. "Isn't that what families do?" she asked finally. "Look out for one another?"

"Lookin' out for one another is one thing, but you…" His voice drifted off uncomfortably.

"I what?"

"Never mind."

"No, I want you to tell me."

"Grandma said it was normal, the thing you have, because of what you'd gone through. Because of your mom and dad dying in that accident when you were only twelve."

"What thing do I have?" Noelle asked. "What

did Grandma say was normal because of what I'd been through?"

He looked like he regretted saying as much as he had.

"It doesn't matter. Let's just forget it. And have fun."

"I don't think I can forget it now."

Rufus looked apologetic. "You have this thing with control. You think you know what's best for everyone."

"I do?" she asked, appalled.

"Ellie, you don't give yourself over to life. You want all your ducks lined up in a row. You want everything the same all the time. I'm scared if you keep it up, you'll end up just like *her*."

They both knew he was talking about Nana.

"She seems like a very nice lady," Noelle said, hearing the stiffness in her voice.

"Oh, sure. All rigid and shrieking and wanting everyone to obey her rules, and scared of wolves hiding under her bed."

"I am not stuck in a rut," Noelle sputtered.

"Look at your room," he said.

She stared at her grandfather. She wanted so badly for what he was saying not to be true. But she thought of Mitchell leaving, flinging words at her over his shoulder as he shoved his skinny underpacked suitcase through the door.

*Nothing's fun with you. Nothing's spontaneous. You can't stand it when I move a chair. We can't go out for dinner without planning for a week. There's no adventure. There's nothing unexpected. I want something else for my life.*

"It's normal," her grandfather said softly, "to want the world to be safe. To feel as if you can have control over the things that make it safe. But you pay a price for it, too."

She could feel her eyes welling.

Her grandfather looked at her imploringly. He didn't want her to be upset. He hadn't wanted to say that, at all. She could tell. It was love for her that had made him say it. She felt as if it might have been what she most needed to hear, even though it was painful.

"I'm sorry," Rufus said.

"It's okay," she said quietly. "I'm glad you told me."

"Let's go back to the house."

"I'm going to stay out here for a little while."

"Are you mad at me?"

"No." That was true. She fished her cell phone out of her pocket and wagged it at him. "I get a bit of service up in the loft. I'll just check on the state of the world."

"Probably limping along without you," her grandfather teased, and then pulled her close and kissed the top of her head in a way that made it all okay.

Noelle went up the rickety ladder and crossed the floor. She opened the loft door and sat down in a pile of sweet-smelling hay. For the longest time she didn't look at her phone, but gazed at the stars in an inky night, contemplating what her grandfather had said.

Finally, a chill began to penetrate even her warm jacket.

She clicked her phone on and looked with annoyance at the no-service symbol. She leaned out the hayloft and held the phone at arm's reach. Two bars. Stretching, she hit one of her social media icons. It was already open on Mitchell's page and she saw he had been updating feverishly. She glanced at the most recent post.

Nearly Christmas and snorkeling. That's what I call living life to the fullest.

A girl who looked too young for him was sharing the selfie.

Noelle felt her throat closing, the tears that had threatened earlier were making a reappearance. *Don't cry*, she told herself, but she did.

"Hello."

She whirled and dropped the phone, thankfully inside and not out the open door.

Aidan reached for her quickly, pulled her away from the loft opening and steadied her, his hand warm and strong on her shoulder. "Don't take a tumble out the window. Would put a terrible damper on all the Christmas cheer."

"Don't sneak up on me!" Noelle wiped hastily at her cheeks.

"I wasn't sneaking," he said reasonably. "I saw the light up here and came to investigate. I thought I made quite a bit of noise. Perhaps whatever you were looking at was totally engrossing?"

He seemed to realize his hand was still on her shoulder. He released her and leaned down, and before she could, swooped up the phone. Instead of handing it back to her, he scowled at the screen.

"I thought you said there was no service."

# CHAPTER EIGHT

REALLY, AIDAN THOUGHT, the right thing to do at the moment would be to hand Noelle her phone and leave her up here by herself. He had obviously interrupted a very private moment. Had she been crying? It was hard to tell in the dim light.

Still, when Noelle made a grab for the phone, Aidan could clearly see, in its faint glow, that her cheeks had little streaks down them. Definite tear tracks remained despite her efforts to scrub them away with her sleeve. He found himself holding the phone out of her reach, unable to not look at what had caused her such distress.

An ordinary-looking chap was on a beach with a girl who looked way too young for him. He had posted something about snorkeling and living life to the fullest.

"Friend of yours?" He carefully stripped his voice of the anger he was feeling that somehow this man had made her cry.

"Ex. Ex-friend, I mean." The truth rode heavy in her tone. Aidan watched her with narrow eyes as she swallowed hard.

Her ex was putting up a seemingly endless series of posts? Gloating about his new life? He held the phone still out of her reach, continuing to study the picture.

"He wanted adventure," Noelle said faintly, reluctantly, almost apologetically.

Aidan remembered, sickened at himself, how he had needled her—could it possibly be just yesterday—about a recent heartbreak. As if it was somehow all about him.

But in such a short time, he had seen the truth of her. Or maybe it was just this setting, but somehow Noelle seemed pure in a world that was tainted, innocent in a world that was sinfully excessive in every way. It was the very purity of her that had to be guarded against, the part of her that called to some forgotten place in him and tempted him to play, to be carefree, to let go a bit.

He had to protect himself from the unexpected *sizzle* she made him feel, not because of her wholesomeness, but in spite of it. He had to ward that awareness off, not just for his sake, but her own.

He'd already disappointed one woman who was far more worldly than Noelle!

Still, he could not stop himself from trying to say something that would make her feel better. "Well, if you call getting a sunburned head an adventure, I'd say he's got it. That's going to hurt like hell."

"We can only hope," she muttered, and he laughed and handed her her phone, which she turned off and put in her pocket.

"For what it's worth," he said softly, "he's missing the greatest adventure of all."

Now where had that come from? His implication was that sharing a life with her would be the greatest adventure of all.

Her mouth opened. And shut. And opened again. Finally a sound squeaked out.

"I'm apparently a bit of a stick-in-the-mud. A controller." She hiccupped. "Even my grandfather said it was true. That's why he didn't tell me about anyone else coming for Christmas. Because he thought I would have tried to wreck it before he even got it off the ground."

"Would you have?"

"Yes."

"Just for his own good," he said gently.

"He said if I wasn't careful I'd end up all rigid and shrieking and wanting everyone to follow my rules."

"Ouch."

"I need to quit meddling. I told you there was no cell service here for your own good, too."

"Not just to be mean?" he teased. He realized he liked teasing her. He liked throwing snowballs at her. He liked making gingerbread houses with her.

"I thought I knew what was best for Tess," Noelle said wistfully. "I thought she needed your undivided attention, without distractions from work. None of my business, right? I'm so certain I know what's right for everyone that I'll lie! It's disgusting."

There was a little trickle of tears sliding down her cheeks again. Couldn't she see how much it meant to him that she cared about Tess like that?

He touched her shoulder. It was so slight under his hand. It made her seem exactly as she was—small, vulnerable, needing him in some way.

To validate her, to protect her, to *see* her. "You have a good, good heart, Ellie McGregor."

Embarrassed, she tried to slide out from under his touch. But he would have none of it. Instead of letting her by, he blocked her way.

When she tilted her head up at him, looking askance, he touched her chin with the tip of his pointer finger and looked at her face.

The fight seemed to leave her. She looked back at him. She looked at him in a way he was not sure he'd ever been looked at before, deeply and intently, as if she was divining secrets about him he did not even know himself.

It felt as if she was turning the tables on him, giving him what he had intended to give her.

He dropped his finger from her chin.

He ordered himself to go, to get away from her. He warned himself he could not be trusted with this kind of innocence, this kind of purity.

But instead of leaving, he put his arms around her and tugged her into his chest, closed his hands on the small of her back and held her tight.

A small mew of protest came from her, followed swiftly by a sigh of surrender. She snuggled into his chest. And then she let go. She wept.

Finally, when the front of his jacket was pretty much soaked, she pulled away from him.

"I'm so sorry. It's been a hard few months. First, my grandfather sold the land. Then my grandmother died. Then Mitchell ended our engagement."

And despite the fact that it had been a hard few months, she had overcome his initial rudeness to her to embrace the needs of his daughter. He thought of how she was working at creating the perfect Christmas, her devotion to it almost fierce.

Aidan Phillips felt something he had not felt for a long, long time. The shame of self-recognition.

He had become a self-centered jerk!

"I should go in," she said uncomfortably, swiping again at her face with her sleeve.

"Don't rush off," he said. "Let's sit for a minute. Look at those stars tonight. I don't remember the last time I paused to look at things. To really see them."

He lowered himself in the hay, and after a moment she sat down beside him, and they looked out the loft door at the humbling largeness of a star-studded universe.

"It's one of the things I always love about coming here," Noelle said. "Life seems simpler, I feel as if I notice small things more—the smell of wood smoke, the feel of the dog's fur under my fingertips, the stars at night."

The quiet of the night, Noelle at his side, the expanse of the universe all stirred in him a stunning desire.

Just to be a better man. Maybe not forever, but for this moment.

"So," he asked her softly, "what do you think made you want to fix all that is wrong in the world? In my experience, people who are like that usually have a reason."

She hesitated. Aidan could tell she didn't

share private things. She was reserved. He was practically a stranger. And yet the invitation of that bejeweled night sky, of a larger world, seemed to be working on her, too.

"My mom and dad died when I was twelve," she said. "That's when I came here to live with Grandma and Grandpa."

"I'm so sorry. How?"

"A car wreck. It was springtime. It seemed as if good weather had come. A freak storm came out of nowhere, and they slid into a truck. They died instantly, which people told me was a blessing.

"And people told me they loved each other so much—which I already knew, of course—and that they had chosen to be together for eternity."

"That's a very thoughtless thing to say," he said gruffly.

She turned to him, her eyes wide.

"Why would you say that?"

"Obviously your mother and father loved you that much, too. They would have never chosen to leave you. What utter clap-trap."

She sighed and leaned into him. "Thank you for saying that."

"I heard it all, too, when Sierra died. People mean well, but honestly, the things they say sometimes! She's in a better place? What better place is there than with your baby? God needed another angel? Her little girl needed a mommy.

"Tess was barely two when her mother died, and I saw how it affected her and still does. The loss of both your parents must have been devastating for you."

"Yes."

Some deep bond of understanding grief connected them.

Then, seemingly randomly, his phone began to ping, as service kicked in and one by one his messages arrived.

He fought a desire to take his phone out of his pocket and hurl it into the night.

"Haven't heard that sound for a while. I can't say I missed it. I thought I would. But I haven't. Amazingly, the world turned without me."

"I think that's what my grandfather was trying to tell me tonight—that life will unfold, whether I have a stranglehold on it or not. Go ahead," she said. "See what's unfolded."

"Not just yet," he said quietly. "Not just yet."

And she leaned her head against his shoulder, and he put his arm around her, and they experienced the glory of the night. But it was cold, and he felt her, after a while, shiver against him.

"Let's go in," he suggested.

"Check your messages first. You never know

when you might get another opportunity. The stars have to line up just so."

It seemed to him the stars had lined up just so tonight, and it had nothing to do with receiving cell service. Still, he did have obligations, and people were counting on him to meet those. He pulled his phone out, reluctant to join the world, liking this one, with its quiet and simplicity and connection, just fine. He scanned the messages very quickly, dismissively.

"Work. Work. Work. Christmas Enchantment Ball. Work. Work."

"The Christmas Enchantment Ball?" she asked.

He scrolled back to the annual ball held each year, always the evening before Christmas Eve, to honor those who gave to charities. "Tomorrow night. The theme this year is Silver Bells."

"I think it's still the biggest event on Calgary's social calendar," Noelle said. "My mom and dad were invited once. It was one of the highlights of my mom's life. She got the invitation because she'd been the top fund-raiser for the children's hospital that year. How do you rate a ticket?"

His company was highly philanthropic, and they were always given a block of tickets. There would probably be thirty people from Wrangler there this year.

"Never underestimate the power of charm and good looks," he said, waggling his eyebrows wickedly at her.

That earned him a smack in the arm, which he rubbed dramatically. She shivered again and he got up and extended his hand to her. She took it, and he pulled her to her feet.

He looked at her. She looked back at him. The stars all seemed to be lining up… She leaned in. He leaned in.

And then his phone pinged, a small sound that sounded like an alarm going off. They leaped back from each other as if Tess had happened upon them.

He looked at his phone, an excuse not to look at her, not to wonder what on earth her lips would taste like. Would they taste as sweet as they looked, like plump dew-encrusted strawberries, fresh from the plant?

He stared intently at the incoming message, at first not even registering what it said. But when it did penetrate, he lifted his shocked eyes to hers.

"Noelle, they found one."

"One what?"

"Guess."

"Jerry?"

"That's it! They found a Jerry Juicejar."

She laughed, sharing his delight and his incredulous disbelief. "It's a Christmas miracle," she teased him. "Of all those messages, even the one about the Christmas Enchantment Ball, that's the one that means the most to you, isn't it?"

"You have no idea," he said, and gave a whoop of pure happiness. "I'll fly in tomorrow and pick him up, then he'll be under the tree waiting for Tess on Christmas morning."

And then it occurred to him. He was being given an opportunity, not just to pick up Jerry Juicejar.

No, maybe it wasn't about that at all.

He was being given an opportunity to be a better man. Not to put his guard up but to let it down, just for a little bit, and just for one shining moment to put her needs ahead of his own. He thought of the wistfulness in her voice when she had mentioned the Christmas Enchantment Ball. He thought of how hard she had been working to make Christmas divine for his thus-far-disappointed-in-the-festivities daughter, despite her own year of losses.

He thought he had just come up with the best Christmas surprise ever. Even the importance of Jerry Juicejar paled in comparison.

"Why don't you come?" he asked softly.

"What? Me?"

He made a point of looking around the empty

hayloft and then back at her. "Sure. Don't you have any last-minute Christmas shopping to do? We could pick up Jerry, do a bit of shopping and go for lunch."

Then I can surprise her with the ball.

She was silent, struggling.

"To be honest, I'm a little afraid of the helicopter," Noelle said, finally. "I hope you won't think I'm hopeless, but I've never flown anywhere, never even been on an airplane. I think it's one of those control things. You can probably see why Mitchell left for greener—"

"Stop it," he ordered her firmly, and then more softly, "You can trust me, Noelle."

Her eyes, as green as moss, as soft as a caress, rested on his face.

It felt as if all those stars in the sky, not to mention his heart, stood still, waiting to decide if he was worthy to give the gift he had just offered.

And was he worthy? Could he be trusted with someone like her? Not if he thought lecherous thoughts about pillaging her lips!

# CHAPTER NINE

NOELLE STARED AT AIDAN.

She had to say no. She had just revealed her deepest heartaches to him. He felt sorry for her. That was what had prompted this invitation.

But perhaps there was a different way to see it. What if it was an opportunity? This was exactly what her grandfather had wanted her to learn: to say yes to life, instead of no. It was an opportunity to get out of her comfort zone! And she needed to take it.

Plus, ever since the tree had gone up in the living room, she had been aware she had no Christmas gifts to put under it for Tess or Nana or Aidan. And she knew the perfect thing to get them!

If she went to Calgary with Aidan, she could get them each a pair of skates so that they all could skate on the pond Christmas morning, a McGregor tradition.

"You know what?" she said. "Yes, I'll come."

It was not as if they were marching off to explore the jungles of South America. They were going to Calgary for an afternoon. In the adventure department it probably barely rated.

Except for the helicopter part.

Except for the Aidan Phillips part.

"Good girl," he said softly.

And just then she realized she did not want him to think of her as a girl, a heartbroken little waif who had been orphaned at twelve. Who wore pajamas with penguins on them and slippers shaped like hairy monsters, and had hardly changed a thing in the room she had had since she was twelve.

That was not how she wanted Aidan Phillips to see her at all. And she was fairly certain, from the way his eyes had rested on her lips a few minutes ago, that maybe that was not how he saw her. Not completely.

"Of course, I'll ask Nana and Tess to come, too. I wouldn't want to deprive Tess of my undivided attention on our holiday."

Why did she feel disappointed, her own words coming back to bite her?

He cocked his head. "What is that noise? Is somebody there?" He stepped in front of her as if he might have to protect her from marauders.

In some ways, it was a very nice feeling to have someone want to protect her. But she had a feeling that Aidan might be trying to protect her from himself, from the attraction that leaped in the air between them. She realized she had told him quite a bit about herself tonight, but she still virtually knew nothing of him. One more excellent reason to go to Calgary with him!

"It's only horses," she said.

"I didn't know there were horses. How have we managed to keep that from Tess?"

"Good question," she murmured. Should she warn him her grandfather was planning a special Christmas surprise? One that would possibly eclipse even the much-coveted Jerry Juicejar?

It seemed much kinder to just let Aidan enjoy his victory in the Christmas dad department.

Or was it simply duplicitous on her part? Considering her initial hesitation in accepting his invitation to join him on his trip to Calgary, she now didn't want to do anything to spoil the moment or put her invitation in jeopardy.

The next morning, Tess announced in no uncertain terms she was not leaving the ranch. She was not leaving her new best friend, Smiley. Nana had promised Christmas cookie baking. She wanted to play outside in the snow.

"I agree," Nana said, seeming pleased by the decision. "It will just make everything simpler if we stay. If you could pick me up a few fresh vegetables, that would be great."

"Noelle? I need to talk to you for a minute."

Noelle's grandfather beckoned her to the hall. He handed her a crumpled roll of bills.

"I wasn't 'spectin' Nana. It would just be rude not to have a present for her. Nothing too personal. No jewelry or anything."

"No, I understand perfectly." But looking at how flustered her grandfather was, she was not certain that she did.

"So much for Tess wanting my undivided attention," Aidan said an hour later, after he had filed his flight plan over the phone and they had gone out to the helicopter. He helped Noelle into it. "She's used to me being away for long periods."

"I actually think she's very secure in your love," Noelle said.

"Huh. I actually think my affections have been replaced by those of a dog. Jerry Juicejar will change all that, though. Take that, Smiley!" Despite making light of it, Noelle could tell it mattered to him that she approved of his parenting. Somehow it felt good that her opinion had value with him.

His good humor, his total lack of nervousness as he went through his preflight checks, helped Noelle feel slightly calmer. Still, when he handed her the earphones her heart was beating way too fast, and her palms were sweating as the engines started and the blades slowly, and then rapidly, began to turn.

"Give me your phone," he said.

She found it in her purse.

"Unlock it."

Was this some sort of aviation requirement? She felt so unsophisticated. She unlocked her phone and handed it to him.

He grinned, flipped through it and found the camera. He aimed it at her. "Give me two thumbs up and a big smile," he instructed.

She did and he took the picture, looked at it and handed it back, pleased.

"Post that on a few of your accounts," he told her.

She laughed out loud, and somehow didn't feel as nervous at all.

As they lifted off the ground, the snow kicked up around them in a cloud. The helicopter seemed to be lumbering. Her hands tightened in a knot on her lap.

But when she glanced at his face for reassurance, Aidan was calm and relaxed. Noelle realized that this came to him as naturally as driving a car did to her.

She looked out her window.

Far below them, already, was the ranch house

and barn. She was stunned by the beauty of this perspective.

"I feel as if I am looking down on one of those large scenes that model rail enthusiasts build," she said in wonder.

"Are you still scared?"

She liked the way his voice sounded, coming straight into her ear from the headphones. "What makes you think I was scared?"

"The pulse beating in your throat? The white knuckles?"

She laughed and unknotted her hands. It added to her sense of wonder that he had observed her so closely, *cared.* "All over being scared," she said.

"Good. Flying is actually safer than being in your own bathroom."

"What?"

"Statistically you are much safer here than in your own bathroom. You'd be astounded by the number of deaths annually in the powder room."

"How?" she said skeptically.

"I'm assuming wet, slippery surfaces, but I'd have to look at the statistics more closely. You aren't supposed to express doubt! You're just supposed to be reassured."

"Humph! Who studies those kinds of statistics?" she asked.

"Nerds, like me."

He was about the furthest thing from a nerd that she could possibly think of, but glancing at him, she realized he already knew that. He didn't need any reassurances from her. He was teasing her. She loved it!

"Getting ready to land," he said.

"That was unbelievably fast."

"Between the higher speed you can attain and the fact that you can travel in pretty much a straight line, it is really fast. It's a very efficient way for me to visit our job sites."

"And you love to fly," she said.

Aidan smiled.

She loved to make him smile.

"Yes, I do."

He had a vehicle in a parking stall reserved for him at the airport. It was a luxury four-wheel drive with a cute little car seat installed in the second row.

It was the antithesis of her little car, and not like anything her grandfather had ever had at the ranch. Mitchell had always liked sports cars—probably an early warning sign that he was looking for adventure. Still, he had not been able to afford new models, so she had never been in a vehicle with a seat warmer built in.

"This is decadent," she said as her seat began to heat up in the vehicle, chilly from being parked so long. "Helicopters, heated seats." She almost said, *A person could get used to this*, but the very thought drew her up short.

She had said yes unexpectedly to an adventure. There was no sense thinking the course of her whole life was changed. That she was in some way tangling with Aidan Phillips in ways that would last. In fact, it would be downright dangerous to indulge in such thoughts.

On the other hand, didn't she overthink everything?

Couldn't she just enjoy this day for exactly what it was? Wasn't that what *adventure* implied? A delight in the moment, in the unexpected, without trying to read the future, plan ahead, figure out everything into the next millennium?

"Jerry has been delivered to my office, so I thought we'd stop in there, and then maybe head to that new mall. I know you probably have your own things you want to do, but I was hoping you'd help me with something. You mentioned all the small things little girls like. What did you say, hair ribbons and teddy bears. New pajamas? Maybe a bracelet?"

"I'd love to help you with that."

His office was at the heart of the steel-and-glass forest that was downtown Calgary. Noelle worked down here herself, so she knew what a nightmare parking was. She took transit.

But he slipped into an underground spot reserved for him, and they took a posh elevator to the top floor.

His office was stunningly elegant: exotic hardwoods, glass, stylish furniture and great art.

He greeted everyone by name, including the maintenance man. He asked after one employee's child by name, asking how the Christmas concert had gone. Noelle could tell his employees didn't just respect him; they revered him.

It was quite a different picture than what Noelle had imagined when she had first met him—she'd seen him as high-powered and cynical. There was another side to him that he was not quick to let people see. She suspected it was an honor that she was seeing it just days after he'd landed in her life.

They went into his office. It was a corner space with floor-to-ceiling windows looking out over the whole city. Should she take a picture of this to post, too? To show what dizzying heights she was dancing with? But somehow, she seemed to have lost her taste for posting her adventures for the public. Wouldn't everyone just see what she realized herself?

"Spectacular," she whispered, but the truth was she didn't feel all that good about it. Instead, she was feeling totally out of her league.

Yes, it was an honor that she was seeing another side of him, but it deepened a sense of inadequacy in her.

He was not the kind of man a girl should fall in love with.

The thought made her heart stand still. Was she falling in love with him? Silly. You could not fall in love in days, could you? In mere hours?

And yet, she felt something for him that was unlike anything she had ever felt before. She had certainly never felt like this with Mitchell—as if her very skin was tingling with aliveness.

"This is what's spectacular!"

He pounced on a package that had been left on his desk.

She looked at the happiness in his face, and again chided herself. Did she always have to be so serious? To the point of being ludicrous?

Of course she was not falling for Aidan Phillips! It was easy to get swept away by helicopters and luxury cars and a fancy office and an entire adoring staff.

"Come look," he said with boyish enthusiasm.

She could not resist. She went over to him and peeked over his shoulder at the package in his hand.

"Oh, my," she said. "Jerry Juicejar is ugly!"

He shouted with laughter, and Noelle looked

at his face, luminous with delight, with joy that he was doing something for his daughter.

"This should make up for Disneyland Disaster," he proclaimed.

And she had to nudge away the thought that whatever she was feeling had very little to do with helicopters and luxury vehicles.

It had to do with cutting down trees and sitting in haylofts and seeing the expression on his face whenever he looked at his daughter.

It had to do with recognizing the value of those moments without any need, whatsoever, to put them in a post to share with the world.

He glanced over his shoulder at her. "What?" he asked.

"Nothing," Noelle said and then added brightly, "We better get on with our shopping. Between the two of us we have quite a bit to accomplish yet."

# CHAPTER TEN

IF NOELLE HAD hoped shopping would prove a distraction to her sudden, uncomfortable and somewhat exhilarating awareness of Aidan, she was wrong.

It was December 23, and the mall was absolutely thronged.

If this bothered Aidan at all, it did not show. In fact, for a man who had seemed cynical about Christmas not so long ago, he was able to give himself over to the shopping chaos with a certain abandon.

He was the rarest of things—a man who was fun to shop with. She could not help noticing how unfailingly respectful he was to the harried sales staff, teasing smiles out of some of them, always dropping a kind remark about how well they were handling the demands of the crowds.

Their arms were soon laden with parcels: hair bows and the most gorgeous teddy bear Noelle had ever seen. The price of it took her breath away, but Aidan paid for it cheerfully. They bought Tess a set of little bangle bracelets, fuzzy Christmas pajamas, the kind with feet in them, and some new storybooks. Everywhere they went they were mistaken for a couple, for a mommy and daddy doing last-minute shopping, and that overlaid the happiness of the experience with faint wistfulness.

While they were in the bookstore, they came across a photo book of exquisite gingerbread houses.

"Rufus asked me to pick out something for Nana. What do you think?"

"Perfect," he agreed. "Nana, check. Tess, check. Now I just need a bit of private shopping time—"

Noelle realized he intended to get her something. She wanted to protest how unnecessary it was, and at the same time she could not. She wanted to see what he would get her!

And, of course, she still needed to shop for her chosen gift of skates for everyone.

"Why don't we meet at Percival's for lunch?" he said. "It's just a short walk from here."

Noelle gulped. Percival's? "Isn't it, um, kind of hard to get in there?"

"I'll figure it out," he said, and then he cocked his head at her and winked. Winked! They probably knew him by first name at the exclusive eatery, where she had never even attempted a reservation.

She scuttled off to finish her shopping, trying not to be too bowled over by the surprises life could hold if you opened your heart just the tiniest bit.

The skates came in huge boxes. Plus, it was a tradition at the ranch to hang a sock on the mantel on Christmas Eve. The tradition continued no matter how old you were. So she didn't just want to hang a sock for Tess, she wanted one for everyone. Noelle threw her slender budget—already strained by the skates, not to mention Mitchell emptying the account—to the wind and bought stocking stuffers of luxury chocolates, pretty envelopes of hot chocolate, colorful mittens, decks of cards and other Christmassy and cute trinkets.

Aidan had arrived before her for lunch but the maître d' was waiting for her to arrive! He guided her to a private table in a small alcove. She plopped herself down at the table, exhausted but happy.

"What have you there?" he asked, reaching for one of her bags. She slapped his hand away.

He pretended to nurse it and they laughed.

"I hope you don't mind. I ordered. I have a few favorites here."

Of course he had favorites at the most exclusive restaurant in town!

After an absurdly delicious lunch, she said, "I think I'm about finished shopping. How about you? Is there anything else you need to do before we fly back to the ranch?"

She couldn't help smiling at that. Plain old Noelle McGregor was sitting in Percival's, after a lunch of crab-stuffed lobster tails, discussing flying back to the ranch as if it was a normal thing. She seemed to have adjusted to the dizzying heights she was visiting, after all.

"There's going to be a bit of a delay in getting back to the ranch," he said.

"There is? Has something come up for you? At work?"

He passed her a slender box across the table. "Not at work exactly. Here. An early Christmas present."

She picked it up, looked at him quizzically, pulled the gorgeous wrapping from it and opened it.

There was a slim leather necklace box inside, the box tastefully embossed from Calgary's number one jeweler.

Her fingers were trembling as she opened it.

Her mouth fell open.

Inside the box was a delicate necklace, with two tiny jewel-encrusted bells on it. Those jewels couldn't really be diamonds, could they? She couldn't see them being fakes, not from that jeweler.

She lifted her eyes to him. "Aidan, I can't take this. It's too much."

"No, you have to take it. It's a way of thanking you for all you've done to give Tess such a perfect Christmas. I called her before you arrived at the table. They made cookies. She and Nana and your Grandpa. She told me about Smiley knocking the cookies off the counter and eating most of them. She was laughing so hard she could barely get the story out. I have not heard my daughter laugh like that in so long. In way too long."

"I wasn't even there! How can you thank me for that?"

"It's not that, specifically. It's all of it. Snowball fights and cutting down trees."

"I don't know," she said uncertainly. "I don't want gifts for it. It's not as if you have to pay me to make a great Christmas for Tess. I like doing it. I want to."

"I'm not paying you. I'm thanking you. Plus, the necklace goes with the theme."

"What theme?"

"Silver Bells."

She cocked her head at him. "I'm not following. I thought you didn't like Christmas carols."

"Despise them," he agreed. "I'm not talking about the Christmas carol called 'Silver Bells.' I'm talking about the Christmas Enchantment Ball. Tonight."

She gulped. "Are you asking me to go to the ball with you?"

He smiled and nodded.

"Like a date?"

He looked slightly taken aback. "I hadn't thought of it in those terms."

*Of course, he hadn't.*

"More like I have tickets, we have some time and when it came up the other night, it sounded like something you might enjoy. Like a little Christmas present."

"But you've already given me the necklace. I can't—"

"One for your birthday, one for Christmas. There's no point to the necklace if we don't go to the ball."

"But we're expected back," Noelle said, feeling faintly panicky. "Tess. And Nana. My Grandpa."

"I'm sure Smiley will miss us, too," he said patiently, "but I cleared it with all of them. They were fine with it. Truth to tell, I don't know if they're going to miss us. I'll still get you home tonight. My helicopter turns into a pumpkin at midnight."

She stared at him. She really did feel like Cinderella. What girl didn't want to be Cinderella once in her life? She fought the impulse.

"I don't know what to say. It's impossible, of course. You'd need a special kind of dress for an event like that." Her voice froze, and it felt as if the fight was draining out of her.

Because she thought of the red dress hanging, never unwrapped, in her closet. That dress didn't have to be a caution against hoping for too much. It could be something else entirely. It could be a statement about saying a bold yes to life and to the adventure.

"I can buy you a dress," he said.

"Actually," she said slowly. "I have one that will do nicely."

"Is that a yes, then?"

She stared at him. She couldn't believe the difference a few hours could make in a life.

"It's a yes," she said, and he let out a hoot of delight much as he had done when Jerry Juice-jar appeared on his desk. The people at other tables smiled indulgently. She supposed to them it looked like more than it was.

A young couple in love. Maybe it looked as if she had said yes to something else.

He leaned toward her.

"You look beautiful when you blush."

She ducked her head and then looked back

at him. Something unfurled inside of her. A great bravery. A wonderful boldness. She felt the shocking jolt of ecstasy from saying yes to the unexpected, to life, to adventure.

Several hours later, she just wasn't as sure. In fact, Noelle felt like she was crumbling like a dried-out Christmas cookie. She had the dress on. Despite the fact that she seemed to have lost some weight, the dress fit like a glove, maybe even better than it had when she first bought it.

The problem was that the dress was shocking.

It was a deep, deep shade of red, like red wine sangria. It was the only designer dress Noelle had ever owned. It was possibly the only dress that had ever taken her breath away. This was the first time she'd put it on since she'd tried it in the store. She remembered the sales lady flitting around her, going into paroxysms of approval.

*For your engagement, you say? It is perfect. It's a girl-to-woman dress, yes?*

Yes, it was that. There were deep Vs at both the front and the back of the dress that were very daring, and didn't allow for a bra. The dress clung in some places and flared in others, and her near nakedness underneath it heightened that feeling of being sensual and being aware of her sensuality, and of leaving the girl behind.

The paleness of her skin became not a detriment but an asset, as if her body had been cast in the finest Versace porcelain.

She had upswept her hair and dusted her features with makeup. Her eyes didn't look murky. They looked like moss, thick and deep, on a forest floor. There was a calm in them that belied how nervous the dress made her feel.

The dress had a red-carpet-ready feel to it. Oh, dear. Was there a red carpet at the Christmas Enchantment Ball? She should look it up. If anybody was bound to trip, it would be her, especially in the unfamiliar two-inch stiletto heels.

She picked up the jewelry box he had given her earlier and opened the lid. She looked longingly at the necklace. If she just put it on, the transformation would be complete, just like Cinderella putting on the glass slipper.

She lifted it out of the box and felt the weight of it, the expense of it.

"Oh, God," she whispered. "Miss McGregor, just who do you think you are?"

Instead of putting on the necklace, she put it back in the box and slammed the lid shut.

Noelle reminded herself tautly she was the woman who had been left. Because she was too predictable. And too controlling. Because she never surprised and avoided spontaneity as if it were the plague. Because she was pale and plain, not golden and exotic.

You couldn't change that! You couldn't change by saying yes instead of no. You couldn't change it with a dress. Or a necklace. Had she lost her mind? She couldn't attend a ball with Aidan Phillips! Every single person would look at her and know she was a fraud, an impersonator, an imposter. They would know that she really wasn't sophisticated enough to pull off a dress like this.

It would show, in the barely-there makeup and in fingers that weren't manicured. And everyone would know that despite the fact that she had been in the city for years, she was still just a girl from the country. Aidan had had her totally pegged in the first few minutes of meeting her. She was wholesome and plain. She had a horrible heartbreak, a betrayal, under her belt. A dress couldn't fix that!

She decided to take the dress off. To put on her housecoat and see if she had any chocolate ice cream left. Aidan could go to the ball by himself.

Or she could get dressed in her old blue jeans and her flannel shirt and they could fly home early if he didn't want to attend by himself. She doubted, though, that he would have a normal person's reticence—read her—about entering such a gathering alone.

Suddenly she just wanted to go home to her grandfather's. She wanted to play with the dog and eat cookies and sit by the crackling fire in her pajamas with penguins all over them. She wanted to try to build that snowman again, on a day with stickier snow, and laugh over ginger-bread houses. And as night fell, she wanted to go sit in the loft, in a cushion of sweet-smelling hay, with the stars studding the sky outside the open loft door. And not to look at social media postings, either.

Her comfort zone. She wanted back into her comfort zone!

Except Aidan Phillips had invaded her com-fort zone, and somehow now, each of those scenarios seemed as if it might feel oddly in-complete if he was not there. If Tess was not there.

There was a knock on the door. There was no doubt it was him. She hadn't ordered pizza. The knock was firm, that of a man sure every door he knocked on would always be opened to him.

She actually looked for a place to hide, but of course, her place was too small to hide any-where. It was a studio apartment. She'd rented it in a reckless effort to leave behind the space she'd shared with Mitchell. She had been will-ing to sacrifice size for the awesome central lo-cation. The tininess had allowed her to get rid of most of the things they had owned together. Thankfully, selling a few quality pieces had brought her some much-needed funds.

But now she could clearly see—looking around her space with its mishmash of used furniture and mismatched dishes—this was not the type of place a dress like this came out of. It was not the impression you wanted to make with a man like Aidan.

She took a deep breath and marched to the door. On her floor tiles, the shoes made a snappy sound like machine-gun fire. Despite the confidence that should have inspired, once she was at the door, her courage failed her completely. She took another deep breath, and then held her nose closed between her thumb and her pointer.

"Aidan?"

"None other."

"I'm not feeling well. You go."

Silence.

"Without me," she expanded.

Silence.

"To the ball."

Silence.

"Have fun!"

Why didn't he say something? He was probably so used to doors being flung open for him that he was in shock. She waited, holding her breath, like a child playing hide-and-seek, try-ing to be invisible, trying not to be caught.

Finally, he spoke. His voice was every bit as firm as his knock had been.

"Open the door, Noelle."

She shivered at the calm in his voice, at the expectation of obedience. "I can't. I want you to go without me. You can come get me when it's done. I'm sure I'll be feeling better in a few hours, ready to go home, ready for—"

"Open the door right now, or I'm kicking it in."

She hesitated. "You wouldn't do that." She forgot to plug her nose.

"Try me," he said.

Really? Aidan Phillips did not seem like the kind of guy you wanted to challenge in that par-ticular way. Where did you get a broken door repaired just before Christmas?

She opened the door. Just a crack. She peered out. "I can't," she reiterated, in her best sick voice, a convincing croak. "You need to go away."

"I'm not going away."

# CHAPTER ELEVEN

*"I'M NOT GOING AWAY."*

Noelle shouldn't really feel as if a statement like that was making her bones melt. After all, it was disrespectful of her right to choose.

And she certainly shouldn't feel shaky and confused and as if her world was upside down. But having the most gorgeous man in the universe standing outside her door, threatening to break it down and then saying in that commanding tone that he was not going anywhere, was not exactly what she had bargained for when she'd decided it was harmless to do things a little differently, to let go of a little control.

There was no sense reading too much into it. *I'm not going away* did not mean Aidan would be around for good. There was no kind of promise of permanence in this evening. It wasn't even a date. He'd been hasty in making that abundantly clear! He'd just stay long enough to stir up her nice, quiet life, to plant seeds of discontent, to leave her testing out a new self without the security of the old one to run back to.

This whole evening had been so ill advised. Why had she said yes? Why had she said he could pick her up here? Now Noelle realized she didn't want him to see her modest studio suite, never mind the dress.

She put her shoulder against the door and pushed, trying to get it closed. It was a metaphor for life. Once you had opened certain doors, it was nearly impossible to close them again.

"Move your foot," she told him.

"No. You don't even sound sick. Were you plugging your nose?"

"Don't be ridiculous. Move your foot, or I'll—"

"Get an ax and chop it off? You did warn me axes were dangerous."

He had no right to be making light of this situation. And the ax? Just a reminder of how different their worlds were.

"I'll call the police."

"Sure you will." His tone was ever so faintly mocking, and ever so faintly gentle. "I'll just slip inside while you go get your phone, because it doesn't really look like you have one hidden anywhere in that dress."

So! He could already tell the dress was inappropriately skimpy. She let go of the door and yanked it open so suddenly he stumbled forward.

"There, are you happy?" she asked him.

He regained his balance quickly. His eyes widened. His jaw went slack. He raked an unsteady hand through his amazing hair.

She stood, feeling terribly undressed. The silence stretched. She tilted her chin at him. Naturally, he looked glorious in a beautifully cut formal tux jacket, a brilliant white linen pleated shirt beneath it. The buttons had been replaced with studs, and the cuffs sported diamond jingle-bells cufflinks that matched the ones on the necklace she had not been able to put on. He had on a red bow tie. It was too bad she wasn't going. That shade of red would have looked very nice with her dress.

He was too big and, naturally, it made her place seem small, as if he filled every inch of it. And he was so sophisticated. He must be looking at her shabby collections with judgment.

"Good God," he said huskily. "Happy? Happy doesn't begin to say it."

"I know," she said. "It's not me. That's why—"

"Do you remember that day we threw snowballs and I told you you were the most beautiful woman I had ever seen?"

As if you could forget something like that!

"I was right," he said, his voice a croak.

He didn't appear to be noticing the humbleness of her surroundings at all. But she could not give in to the softness that made her feel toward him, as if she should just lean in and welcome whatever happened next.

"I'm not beautiful," Noelle said. "In fact I feel utterly ridiculous. I feel like a little girl pretending to be a grown-up. I feel like a fraud. Look around. Does a dress like this come from such a place?"

He looked around, a perfunctory glance that did not take in the chipped teapot at the center of her small table, or the handmade curtains, the mismatched kitchen chairs.

His gaze came back to her and something angry and fierce snapped in his eyes. "You know what? He played on all those insecurities of yours. He made you feel less and less and less. For God's sake, take yourself back."

She stared at him.

"Where's the necklace?"

Noelle felt frozen. Impatient, he glanced around, strode over to the table where she had set the box and picked it up. He came back to her.

"I—I—I changed my mind. I can't accept it."

"Turn around," he growled.

She felt surrender shiver along her spine as she turned her back to him and lifted the few tendrils of hair that had escaped down her neck.

He didn't fasten the necklace, not right away. Instead, he slowly scraped the line of her neck with his finger. She quivered from the pure and heated sensuality of his touch. He stroked her again, his palm this time, sliding over the back of her neck, possessively, leashed desire radiating from his touch.

She closed her eyes. She felt herself sink into his hand, her body sway. The necklace settled on her skin, rode slightly above the deep dip of her cleavage. The bells were heated from where his hands had held them.

He turned her around, traced the line of the necklace to the delicate swell of her breast, then let his hand fall away. He combed his hair with it.

She wished he wouldn't do that. It caused inordinate weakness in her. Her knees felt as if they might buckle.

"It's not up to me to make you feel beautiful, Noelle," he said softly, his voice stern, formidable. "It's an inside job. But it starts like this—it starts with you putting your hand through my arm and holding your head up high and recognizing you deserve to feel your own value.

"Beautiful women are a dime a dozen. Women who shine from the inside out, like you do? That's rarer than the blue diamonds in that necklace."

"Blue diamonds," she stammered. "Aidan, I don't think—"

He raised an eyebrow. He crooked his arm to her.

She hesitated, took a deep breath, took that one step toward him and then threaded her arm through his.

She instantly felt his strength. And her own.

"It's a party," he said, tilting his head to gaze at her. "It's a frivolous, fun evening. It's not a panel of judges eyeing your outfit and your performance. Though even if they did, you'd be a perfect ten."

She could feel the steadiness of his arm entwined with hers. It felt like he was a man you could lean on when your own courage failed.

"That helps put it in perspective," she said, managing a tremulous smile. "It really does. Thanks for talking me back from the edge."

"I didn't talk you back from the edge, Noelle. When you're on the edge, you either turn back or jump."

"I'm not sure I want to jump off any edges!"

"Really? How else do you figure out if you can fly? You might not want to, but you already did tonight."

"Were you really going to kick the door in?"

"Oh, yeah."

"I think I could love it that you're masterful."

"Yeah, at times. It would probably get old after about three seconds."

And then they were both laughing, and she felt giddy, like a child who had jumped off the high diving board for the very first time.

But instead of hitting the water, she had found she had wings. She had found she could fly.

They stepped outside. The cold should have hit her like a brick, but instead she felt warmed through. Besides, she wouldn't be outside for long. She tried not to gape at the vehicle double-parked at the curb.

"A stretch limo?" Noelle asked. "Seriously?"

Her neighbors, in this working-class community of elegant old houses that had been cut up into multiple suites, were sneaking peeks out their windows.

A uniformed chauffeur came and opened the door for her, tipping his cap as she slid by him. Aidan took the seat next to her. He seemed quite at home in the limo. He knew exactly where the chilled champagne was kept!

"You seem to know your way around a limo," Noelle said.

"I guess I do. There won't be any parking for miles around the venue. And Sierra taught me you can't ask a lady in an extraordinarily sexy dress and high heels to walk ten blocks in the cold."

It was a reminder that he knew a lot about this intimidating world they were headed into. And it was a reminder Aidan Phillips had had another life. He'd landed on her grandfather's ranch with his share of baggage, none of which he had offered to share with Noelle.

It was the first time since the morning they had met that he had mentioned Sierra. Noelle hoped she had an opportunity, and soon, to find out why he and Tess were such an island at Christmas. Surely they had family? If he didn't, Sierra must have? Where were the aunts and uncles, brothers and sisters, cousins?

"When you are in the public eye," Aidan said softly, "someone is always watching. For the mistake. For the misstep. And in this day and age they almost always have a camera."

"Yikes," she said. "I hope I'm not going to prove to be the misstep."

"Relax," he said. "Champagne?"

"Half a flute. Just so I can say I did it. Drank champagne in a limo. Lives of the rich and famous and all that."

He laughed and complied, handing her the glass. The bubbles got in her nose. Her nervousness fled, not because of the champagne, but because he had no nervousness at all. He was going to this event in the same way he flew a helicopter: calm and confident.

"No champagne for you?" she asked.

"Not if I'm going to fly later."

"You remind me of a cat," she said. "Relaxed, but ready, too."

He lifted a wicked eyebrow at her and twirled an imaginary moustache. "You never know when a mouse will come along."

The limo slid into a line at one of Calgary's oldest and poshest downtown hotels. Flashes from cameras were lighting the night. There was a red carpet.

She looked at some of the other people getting out of their vehicles. It wasn't like Hollywood. It wasn't like many of them were recognizable. She had just begun to relax when she noticed something.

People went up the red carpet and then congregated at the huge glass doors of the hotel, greeting friends, exchanging handshakes and super-sophisticated busses on proffered cheeks.

"Oh, my God, Aidan, we have to get out of here."

"We just got here." He followed her gaze. "Don't worry. I won't let anyone kiss you."

"I'm not worried about getting kissed."

"Oh, good," he said. "Still, I think I'll save that pleasure for myself."

She wanted to remind him, a little churlishly, that it wasn't even a date. And she wanted to get out of here. Whatever had possessed her to agree to this?

"What's wrong?" he asked, his voice low, picking up on her distress.

"Look at the dresses."

He peered at them. "Nice. Not one holds a candle to yours, though."

"There's a reason for that. Candle. Think candle."

"I don't follow."

"Candles are red. Flame red."

Aidan looked again. "Oh, I see where you're going with this."

"Everyone is wearing silver. Every. Single. Woman."

"All the better," he said gleefully, not understanding the enormity of the fashion faux pas at all. "It's like art. It's your turn to be the star. Your turn to do exactly what you've been avoiding your entire life. Your turn to stand out."

Their car stopped. The chauffeur was out, holding open the door for them. Aidan held out his hand.

She looked at it for a long time, and then tentatively she took it.

"Own it," he mouthed at her.

He helped her from the car, and she stood there, feeling the boldness of the color against the silver of the winter night.

Flashes went off.

She set her shoulders and tilted her chin. Aidan put his hand around her waist, possessively.

There was a faint pattering of applause, as if people approved of her breaking the tradition, standing out, being herself.

"Own it," he told her again, his voice husky in her ear, his breath a sensual touch on the nakedness of her neck.

And so she did. With poise she would not have known was part of her, she slipped her one arm through his, raised her other in a friendly wave to those lined up behind the barriers. She tilted her chin and smiled.

Noelle McGregor felt glorious.

Not just because she had on a gorgeous red dress.

Not because she was a light in a sea of silver.

But because she had faced something inside of her. She had faced that little voice that said, *You are not good enough.*

And she had banished it.

And that made her feel worthy of the glorious man who stood beside her.

# CHAPTER TWELVE

THE CHRISTMAS ENCHANTMENT BALL had been aptly named. Noelle felt as if she was walking into a fairy tale.

An ordinary, large conference room had been totally transformed into a winter ballroom. An illusion of it being outdoors had been created, with huge Douglas fir trees lining both sides of the room. All ten feet high and identical, as if they had been cloned, they could have been mistaken for artificial trees, except for the heavenly smell in the room. The firs sparkled with millions of tiny white lights and glittering silver ornaments so abundant you could barely tell they had branches.

The lighting was actually causing an optical illusion, as if giant snowflakes were falling inside the room. The dance floor was empty, as of yet, but there were clusters of glamorous people milling about, beginning to find their way to tables nestled amongst the trees.

The women's gowns were jaw-dropping. Expensive—all in theme, all silver—jewelry dripped from fingers and wrists and necks.

A low murmur of chatter, laughter, filled the room.

Aidan was well-known and almost immediately swamped. She would never remember all the names of the people he introduced her to. He snagged another glass of champagne off a passing tray for her, and asked the server to bring him back a juice when it was convenient.

"Noelle?"

It was the last place she expected to see anyone she knew, but there was Gerald Simpson, the owner of the small oil field supply company Mitchell had worked for. Though she and Mitchell had attended a number of company functions she was astounded that he even knew her name. The Alberta oil patch really was a very small interwoven community.

Gerald introduced his wife, but when she went to introduce Aidan, he said, "No introductions necessary. I'd be interested in your take on our provincial government, Mr. Phillips."

Noelle was frankly relieved he said that instead of mentioning Mitchell, but she also wondered if this was how the evening would go: networking, contacts, shoptalk.

But Aidan put a stop to it instantly. "I'd love to discuss that with you sometime, Mr. Simpson, but I hear the band starting and I've been dying to have a dance with Miss McGregor."

Dying? Really?

It was early in the evening. No one was on the dance floor yet. They were milling about in glamorous circles, and three deep at the bar.

"No one's dancing," she whispered as Aidan took her glass from her and set it down on the nearest table.

"I know," he said. "Isn't that great?"

Great? It meant everyone would be watching. It meant that she would be in her least favorite position, the center of attention!

"I like this song," he told her. The band was doing a really good cover of an Adele song. Aidan took her hand and tugged her out to the very middle of the dance floor. He faced her. She faced him. He took one of her hands in his, and tucked it close to his chest. He put his other on her hip.

He never looked away from her.

His hand on her hip, and the way his blue eyes rested on her face—intense, seductive, charmed, captivated—might have been just about the sexiest thing she had ever experienced in her entire life. Until he began to dance, that was.

This was one thing she would not have ever

imagined about him. He was a great dancer. If she was out of practice, and not quite so great as him, it never showed. Because he was so graceful and so confident, so comfortable with his body. He was so good at creating an amazing world that held just the two of them. Soon, she totally forgot that others might be watching. They shut out the whole world.

Hips swaying, chests brushing, the distance between them closing and opening up again, the music swirling around them like a wave that they were destined to ride.

"Can I cut in?"

She saw Aidan frown. It was one of the people he had introduced her to when they had first come in. The vice president of his company? Mike Someone?

With ill grace he let her go.

"Where on earth did that lucky dog find you?" Mike asked her.

"Under the Christmas tree," she said with a laugh.

Soon Aidan claimed her back, but then another of his coworkers came and asked to cut in. From these little interchanges she learned a lot about Aidan. It confirmed what she had seen in his office when she had been there briefly with him this afternoon. His people respected him, but they loved him, too. They liked to have fun, and there was lots of good-natured teasing between them. He encouraged that.

And she also had the feeling she was being vetted by them to see if she was worthy of the boss they clearly adored.

The evening was exhilarating. Noelle had never felt so beautiful, so much like a princess. She could not believe how quickly the time flew. Suddenly, it was midnight—hadn't he promised to get her home before midnight, lest his means of transport turned into a pumpkin—and the last dance was being announced.

"May I have the last dance?" he said, bowing to her. It was courtly and old-world and charming, and he didn't seem to care who was watching.

"You may," she whispered.

Aidan took Noelle's hand. He had thought, from the moment he first entertained the notion, that the Christmas Enchantment Ball was a gift to Noelle.

But from the moment she had opened the door of her tiny studio suite, he had known that was not the case at all.

Bringing Noelle to the ball was a gift to himself.

It was the first time he'd taken a woman out since the death of his wife.

And what a woman he had chosen! Being with Noelle was like watching a bud of a rose unfurling to its full glory. He'd watched her go from being shy and awkward in that dress, which was a different color than everyone else's, to owning the dress, and her own beauty, completely. It was an astonishing metamorphosis.

Noelle was each of the things he had always known her to be: wholesome, giving, pure somehow. But now he could clearly see that there was a hidden layer, a depth of passion that was her secret, and which she had saved for just the right man.

And tonight, it was her gift to him, to Aidan, that he was the right man, the one who was there when she awakened fully to her power and beauty and sensuality. The one who was there when she owned all the sides of herself.

Every man in the room saw it in her, her confidence and her hunger, and they were drawn to her like bees to the opened flower that she was.

And yet, as he took her hand for the last dance, he felt her giving this gift into his keeping exclusively. Something tried to nudge him, to warn him to keep a distance, but he chased all the voices away.

He had always been ruled by reason, and he

could see the delicious irony that it was this wholesome woman from the country who was making him just embrace the moment, in all its exquisite glory. And its exquisite glory was awareness of her, so sharp it was almost painful, so heady it was more intoxicating than champagne, so complete it made him feel as if he was full to the top and then overflowing.

He took her hand and led her right to the middle of the dance floor again, just as he had for the first dance.

He knew they were both exhilarated and exhausted by the evening, that neither of them could believe how quickly it had gone by or what a wonderful time they had had.

They waited, gazing at each other for the music to start.

The song that began to play was Canadian music icon Anne Murray's "Could I Have This Dance."

"Could I?" Aidan asked gruffly.

She mock-curtsied to him and took his proffered hand. He drew her close, closer than he had for any other dance. He rested his chin on top of her head, and they swayed together to the beautiful song. He was suddenly aware of how little she had on under the dress, and that rather than making her feel self-conscious, it made her feel all grown-up, sexy, desirable.

It felt as if the song was being sung just for them, as if each question was being asked of them, as if each observation was being made by them.

The music ended.

Still they stood, looking at one another. Aidan dropped his head over hers and claimed her mouth.

His lips were tender on hers. The world faded. It was just the two of them, in a winter fairy tale. He could tell she loved his taste, his scent, his touch as much as he loved hers. Her lips parted even more...

And then he broke away, and felt the shock of it. In his well-planned life, this was an unplanned moment, in the middle of a crowded room. He had not expected this.

To feel so alive again, after such a long time of allowing himself only one feeling: the victory of success in his chosen field.

It took them a long time to leave, saying goodbye to everyone, getting stopped by so many people along the way.

But finally they were outside.

To find a complete enchantment. Snowflakes as big as feathers were falling from the sky.

A complete enchantment unless, of course, you had been planning on flying a helicopter.

It seemed to him the fates had chosen to laugh at him when he most needed control.

Noelle watched as Aidan whipped his phone out of his pocket before taking off his jacket and settling it around her shoulders.

It was still warm from him as if it had been heated in an oven. Noelle wondered if she should object, but then she snuggled in his jacket and the old-fashioned concept of chivalry.

"My grandmother used to say snowflakes were angel kisses."

"Where did this come from?" He scowled as he glared at his phone. He didn't appear to have heard her remark. He flicked to the weather. "It's not even showing it snowing."

She lifted her face and felt the kisses land, wet and delightful on her cheeks. Her sense of magic in the air increased. Apparently his did not. She watched him run a hand through his hair, sending snowflakes flying.

She reached up and tucked a stray strand back into place. It felt exactly as she had known it would from the very first moment she had dreamed of doing it. Just right.

"We can't fly in this," he said. "We'll have to wait and see if it clears."

They were so, so different. She saw angel

kisses; he saw obstacles getting in the way of what he wanted.

And yet, maybe because of the magic they had just shared, she saw their differences could be good things. Life was about balance, wasn't it?

Her elbow firmly in his hand, she began to navigate the steps that had not been snow-covered when they came up them. Unfortunately, her shoes were not intended for slippery conditions. Her foot slipped out from under her and her ankle twisted.

She probably would have tumbled right down the steps if his reflexes had not been so swift, his hold on her elbow so strong.

"Lean on me," he said. And then he practically carried her to the waiting limo. She was not even sure how he knew which one it was; there were so many limos here.

But he didn't give her address to the driver, he gave his own.

"Did you want to drop me at home?" she asked, thinking he must have overlooked the fact that she needed to go home.

"Why don't we go to my place? I don't want to leave you on your own with a possible twist to your ankle. As soon as it clears, we'll make a run to your place and pick up what you need to go back to the ranch. I'm afraid—" he squinted out his window "—it may be morning before we can go."

He was inviting her to his place. The circumstances were hardly romantic. She should insist she would be fine on her own.

But the temptation to see where he lived—and how—was just too great. She settled back in the deep luxury of the limo cushions and watched as they sped through a night that was turning from magically snow-filled to a full-blown blizzard.

Aidan lived on the top floor of one of Calgary's premier downtown condominiums. Though it was only blocks from her own apartment, it was a different world entirely. Noelle had read the starting price to get into one of these units was over three million dollars.

It was wonderful to ride up a private elevator, to exit into a plush living room with floor-to-ceiling windows that looked out on the Calgary downtown skyline and the dark ribbon of water that was the Bow River.

The decor was like something out of a magazine: low-slung white leather furniture, shaggy area carpets, an open concept plan with a huge granite island with stools around it, a high-tech kitchen beyond that.

But the space seemed so very sophisticated, adult. Christmas had been ignored. There was no tree, and no decorations up. A single child-ish drawing of Santa had been attached to the stainless steel fridge with a magnet.

"No wonder you can't have a puppy," Noelle murmured. "Where on earth does Tess play?"

Even before Noelle spoke, Aidan felt as if he was looking at his space with vision altered by his few days on the ranch.

It didn't seem friendly, at all, never mind child-friendly.

"Tess plays wherever she wants," he said, and heard a bit of a defensive note in his voice. "The housekeeper has been in. That's why there are no toys about."

"The housekeeper," Noelle echoed.

"You've gotten wet," he said. "You're shivering. It's late. Do you want me to show you a room? Are you tired?"

"Not really. I feel a little wound up still. What a wonderful evening. I can't thank you enough. I should call Grandpa, though, and let him know we will be delayed."

"You're not concerned about waking him?"

"I'm more concerned about him worrying."

It had been a wonderful evening. He felt reluctant to let it go. Did she, too? Somehow this *feeling* he had wasn't part of what he'd bargained for when he'd thought of giving her this gift.

The feeling of being aware of her. That dress had taken his awareness to a new level, and then dancing with her, touching her, watching her awaken to her own glorious sensuality and power had intensified it even further. He was totally bewitched. He had to get her out of that dress, and not in the way a man would normally be thinking of doing with a beautiful woman!

"Why don't I find you some dry clothes, and we'll have a hot chocolate before we turn in. I need to check weather forecasts."

He found her one of his T-shirts and a pair of his pajama bottoms and showed her the guest-room. He noticed she was still limping slightly as she went to put them on.

When she emerged again, he realized getting her out of the red dress had not accomplished what he wanted. At all. Who could have antici-pated that she would look more beautiful in an oversize T-shirt than she had in that stunningly spectacular dress?

After she made her phone call, she sat down on his sofa, curled her feet under her and took a sip of her cocoa. There was a little dot of cream on her lip. He hurried off to find ice for her ankle and made her set it on it. She glanced around and blew on the hot chocolate.

"What?" he asked.

"This space doesn't seem like you," she said, after a moment's hesitation. "Or Tess."

He debated sitting on the couch beside her, but opted for the much safer chair across from her. "I lived here before I met Sierra. When we were married, she brought in a designer. After the fire, I had the option of moving, or doing things differently, but it was suggested to me that Tess needed to come back to familiar surroundings, not something brand-new. I didn't want to feel as if I was erasing her mother from her life."

He could see the way Noelle was looking at him. Though he had kept his tone neutral and tried to strip his words of emotion, something had betrayed him. He'd given away one of his secrets. He had a feeling that Noelle McGregor could divine secrets the way a water witcher could find water. She was looking at him now as if she *knew* he'd been unhappy, as if she knew something had not been quite right in a relationship that had been so carefully and consistently portrayed as perfect.

Or perhaps it was the decor that had given away something. It was so unlike the ranch, so unlike Noelle's own cluttered, but friendly, little apartment.

This space struck him as being like the movie sets his wife was so familiar with. It created an illusion of a home, without quite ever being a home.

"I don't understand why there are no decorations up," Noelle said, probing the secret.

"We're never here at Christmas." Aidan made his voice cool, uninviting.

But Noelle was looking at him with a softness that threatened his every hard edge, that shone like a beacon beckoning him home from stormy seas.

"Why are you and Tess so alone at Christmas? Where's your family? Where's Sierra's family?"

"It's been such a good night," he said. "Maybe we shouldn't—"

"You know how you told me I could trust you in the helicopter? I did, and I don't regret it. I discovered I'm braver than I think."

She gazed at him, not saying the obvious. She was requiring bravery and trust from him, also. A different kind of bravery and trust. She looked adorable in his T-shirt, the pajama pants swimming on her, her feet tucked up under her, the ice pack sliding off her slightly swollen ankle.

She had washed off her makeup and let her hair down.

Her eyes were as deeply green as a shaded place in the forest. He hadn't known her very long. And yet, he felt as if he could trust her as much as he had ever trusted anyone. Had he ever told anyone of these dark secrets in his heart?

No.

And suddenly, looking at her, he felt a terrible weakness. To tell someone. To trust someone with it. To not be so alone in the whole world. He had always felt alone. Even when he was with Sierra. Even though he had hoped for something different.

"You know that day you put up the wreath, and I saw that word? *Hope?* I told you that hope was the most dangerous thing of all?"

"Yes, I've had trouble forgetting that."

"I'm not saying this because I want your pity, or *Oh, poor you*, but I was an only child, an accident, I suspect."

She gasped, and he smiled wearily at her.

"My mom and dad never stopped fighting. Christmas would come, and every single gift I asked for would be given—bicycles or expensive game consoles, the best clothes, the greatest sports shoes. Our whole living room would be filled with gifts. It *looked* like the perfect Christmas.

"But I only wanted one thing—please, stop fighting. That's what I hoped for. Prayed for, even. I'd watch all the Christmas movies and listen to the songs, and they all promised the same thing. It was practically a guarantee that everything that was wrong would somehow become right at Christmas. Even cannons would stop firing and men at war would put down their guns and go meet one another.

"But the war in our house never stopped. My parents finally divorced—thank God—when I was eight. My memories of family were of fighting, and then after the divorce, being used as a club for my mother and father to smack each other with.

"And so, when I met Sierra and we loved each other so fiercely, I thought we could do it differently. Looking back with a tiny bit of the maturity that I wish I'd had then, I realize neither of us came from happy families. Sierra wouldn't even talk about hers. She made up her name to cut any link with them."

Her eyes followed his hand as he raked his hair. He remembered her fingertips in it earlier. He wanted to stop talking, but for some reason he could not explain, the memory of her fingertips in his hair kept him speaking.

"Looking back, what chance could two people coming from histories like that have? We had a whirlwind romance. From the moment I met her, I felt bowled over. When we discovered she was pregnant, just weeks after we met, we were excited. We wanted to get married. We *hoped* we would become the family we dreamed of. Maybe we were even frantic to be that family. Had we waited, we might have discovered we simply didn't have what it took."

"I'm sorry."

"Don't get me wrong. She was a beautiful, vivacious woman. But complicated, in the way highly gifted people sometimes are. I felt like I stole her life force from her, without knowing how I was doing it. I couldn't seem to make her happy. I started spending more time away from her. She felt lonely, I guess, and misunderstood. She started drinking…and worse. We began having fights that could rival anything my parents had ever had. We managed to keep our deep dysfunction secret from the press—never underestimate the power of a good press secretary. The night of the fire—Christmas Eve—we'd had a tremendous row.

"Tess woke up crying. All I could think was *We're doing to this poor kid what was done to us.* I couldn't make Sierra calm down. So I took Tess and I left.

"Sierra didn't normally smoke, never in public. But if she felt stressed, or started drinking, she smoked. The fire investigation said it was a cigarette.

"It never got out to the public that Tess and

I weren't there. The public perception of us as the perfect fairy-tale couple remained intact. It makes all of it, somehow, even harder to bear."

"I'm so sorry." Her voice was soft, a caress of pure compassion.

He lifted a shoulder. He wanted to stop, but somehow he could not, as if he was a train running down a track with no one in control. He hated that the most, being out of control.

"I never even heard from her family, not even when she died. I had a private detective track them down. I wasn't sure if they should know about Tess or not."

"And?"

"Not," he said wearily.

"And your own mother and father? They don't see Tess?"

"My father died before she was born. My mother married a man who lives in Australia. She sends a card and a gift. Now and then she calls. She told me she's way too young to have someone call her Grandma. Tess calls her Peggy."

"Now I know why you think hope is the most dangerous thing," she said. Her eyes were sparkling, as if she was holding back unshed tears. It did not feel like she pitied him. It felt like the truest empathy he had ever experienced.

The train running down the track did not result in a wreck, but in something else entirely unexpected. His heart felt open in a way he was fairly certain it never had been before.

Maybe it was like some kind of a Christmas miracle.

# CHAPTER THIRTEEN

"YOU'RE THE ONLY person I've ever said that to," Aidan heard himself admit slowly. "I don't know if I should have."

But there was something about her, from the green of her eyes to her belief in angel kisses, that invited confidences. Or weakness, depending how you looked at it.

"Why?" Noelle's voice was as soft as the relentless snowflakes drifting down outside his window.

"It feels like a betrayal of Sierra. Of her memory. Tess doesn't really remember her, so I've kind of created this perfect Mommy for her to remember."

"That doesn't sound like something a true cynic would do."

"Sometimes I even surprise myself," he admitted. "Like sharing this tonight. That's a surprise."

"Maybe it's just a weight you've carried by yourself for too long."

He waited to feel the shame of having let his guard down, of having let out secrets that he should not have, the guilt at his loss of control.

Instead, looking at Noelle, he felt she was right. He felt a new lightness, as if he had carried a burden for too long.

And he also felt exhausted.

"I'll show you where you're going to sleep tonight."

"Not just yet," she said softly. She patted the sofa beside her.

He knew he should resist this. He knew it. And yet he was not that strong. He got up from his own chair and went and sat beside her.

"Closer," she said, her voice soft but firm.

He moved toward her, until his leg was touching her leg, until the length of his side was pressed against the length of her side, fused. Her hand took his.

She lifted it to her lips and then lowered it to her lap, stroking it, all the while saying nothing. She did not try to fix or pry.

And yet he felt her tenderness, her compassion, the purity of her beautiful spirit in that featherlight touch on his hand.

"Thank you," he said gruffly.

He did not resist when she guided his head to her shoulder, when she traced the plains of his face with her fingertips, healing in her touch.

Something in him that he did not know he held in constant tension unraveled. Her breath deepened, and so did his. He marveled that he felt as deeply relaxed as he had ever felt.

No, something more than relaxed.

He felt safe.

In Noelle's touch, in her total and unconditional acceptance of him, Aidan felt as if he had finally, finally found his way back to a place he had never really been: home.

He wasn't sure how long he was there, but her voice came to him through a thick haze.

"Aidan, you are going to get a sore neck. Go to bed."

He rose and stared down at her, and then held out his hand. She took it, and he pulled her gently to her feet. The bag of partially melted ice that had been on her ankle splatted to the floor.

She went to pick it up, but he did not want such a mundane thing to break the magic between them.

"Leave it," he insisted.

He led her down the hall to his bedroom, through the door, to the luxurious largeness of his bed. He pulled back the sheets with one hand, holding her hand tight with the other.

Then he turned and looked at her. Faint light was washing through the window, washing her in the silver enchantment that had shivered through the whole evening. She looked at him, wide-eyed, willing for whatever came next in a way that made him slightly ashamed, that called on him to be the better man.

"Let me just hold you," he said gruffly.

Her expression relaxed into a mixture of disappointment and relief that made him feel, with abundant clarity, it had been the right decision.

Slipping into the bed beside her, pulling her fully clothed body against his own. Feeling her breath on his chest and her hair tickle his chin, her scent waft up to his nostrils, her softness filling all his emptiness, Aidan felt like for once he was the man he had always wanted to be.

Noelle woke to soft light, muted gray falling across her face. For a moment she felt disoriented, but then she felt Aidan's arm over her midriff, heavy and possessive, in a way that made her heart feel full. His scent filled her with euphoria like a forbidden drug, one that once you had it, you could never ever get enough.

She took advantage of the fact that he still slept to study his face, dark whiskers, his hair falling over his brow.

After a while, she became aware of other things. The massive bed they shared could easily be a single size, they were cuddled so close together. The room was as beautiful as the rest of his space, but as beautiful as it was, it was impersonal, like a hotel room. Where were the photos and the socks on the floor? Where was Aunt Bessie's old wardrobe, the framed art of a child? Somehow there was no history here, and none of his dynamic personality. It made her acutely aware that all his success was driven by a need to outrun the loneliness of his own heart.

Out the window the huge snowflakes still fell. Her sense of well-being left her. It was still snowing. And it was Christmas Eve. She touched his shoulder, and he pressed against her hand, buried his face in her neck. She took a deep breath and nudged more firmly.

His eyes flashed open. So blue. Full of tenderness. Welcome.

"Noelle," he said, his voice a purr of pure seduction.

Easy to want to follow it to wherever temptation led, but no. It was Christmas Eve. They had responsibilities.

"Look at the weather," she said to him.

His eyes narrowed on her face, and then he looked over her shoulder. He rolled away from her, was out of the bed in one lithe move, and went to the window. He opened the curtain fully.

And said a word she had not heard him use before.

It was when he turned back to her that she knew, somehow, someway, that without her permission, following the trail of breadcrumbs life had put out for her, she had come to this.

She loved this man. It was crazy. And stupid. Their worlds were a million miles apart. It was too fast. She had no idea where this was all going. Just like in the story of Cinderella, midnight loomed. Only their midnight was Christmas. He was sharing his life with her until just after Christmas. Then what?

And even with all these rational thoughts crowding around her, Noelle loved him for the panic on his face that she read correctly even before he spoke it.

"It's Christmas Eve. Tess needs me to be with her."

"I know," she said softly.

"Believe it or not," he said, "I am my little girl's Santa Claus and despite my hard-earned cynicism about everything Christmas, I take that responsibility very seriously. I don't ever want Tess to be as cynical about the season as I am. Jerry Juicejar has to have magically appeared under the Christmas tree tomorrow."

"I know," Noelle said.

"I'll drive."

"Of course," she said. She saw it. The fierceness in him. The warrior. With the tender heart.

That he would do whatever it took to be with his daughter on this day, especially, that held so many bad memories for them.

"Look, it might be tense," he said. "I'm sure driving conditions will be abysmal."

"I know."

"You don't have to come."

But, of course, she did. The option of spending Christmas Eve, and no doubt Christmas, by herself was untenable.

"This has got to bring up painful fears for you," he said.

"It does. I have avoided bad roads ever since my parents' accident."

He nodded.

"I've avoided a lot of things. I'm not going to let fear rule me anymore," she said. And she meant it.

And so, when they headed out an hour later, she had a sense, not of being afraid, but of tackling a great adventure with a man she trusted. After his confidences last night she trusted him more than ever. And she had admitted her secret love for him. Once again, doubts crowded. But she shoved them away, determined to cherish these moments.

Telling herself that love made everything possible. Even the impossible.

The vehicle was a good one, a heavy-duty

four-wheel drive, the kind that had been invented for the military but adapted to civilian use.

They piled all their gifts in it. And a thermos of coffee. Snacks. Extra clothing. A car blanket. An emergency kit with a flashlight and a candle, matches and first-aid equipment.

The primary highway south of Calgary, while not in the best of condition, was passable. The plows and sanding trucks were working full force to help keep the roads safe for people anxious, as Noelle and Aidan were, to be with loved ones for Christmas.

The vehicle felt solid and safe, but Noelle was aware her sense of safety came as much from Aidan as from the vehicle. Aidan drove the same way he flew a helicopter, with the great calm and confidence of a man certain of his own strengths and abilities.

They listened to music and chatted easily. He made her laugh out loud with stories of Tess and his own bumbling through single parenthood. She told him of coming, as a child of the city, to live with her grandmother and grandfather on their ranch, and how she had come to love it. They argued playfully about music choices and favorite movies and TV shows.

She felt so relaxed—and truthfully, nursing her secret love for him, happy to have this time alone with him—that she could scarcely believe a storm raged outside the capsule of warmth and laughter and safety that they shared.

It was when they turned off the main road and onto the secondary highway that conditions deteriorated. The road crews were not giving the secondary roads the same priority, and the storm seemed to thicken around them. The little traffic there was crawled along, back tires slithering.

And then in the line of cars in front of them, the brake lights of a small blue car flashed red in the storm. Noelle and Aidan watched helplessly as a deer, followed by another, darted out in front of it. The car avoided the deer, but lost control and swung around in several looping circles before going off the road, its snub nose buried in a snowdrift. The cars behind it avoided collision, but once they regained traction, they kept going.

Only Aidan pulled well off the road. "Stay here," he told her.

Watching him push his way to the car and lean in to talk to the driver, she was overcome with a sense of admiration for him. Despite all he had been through—a terrible childhood and a disappointing marriage and the death of his partner—this was still who he really was. Decent and honorable. The one who could be counted on to stop, even in the middle of a storm, and do the right thing.

He claimed cynicism, but underneath that was the heart of a good man, and a strong one. One able, in challenging circumstances, to make the right decision, to be better for the things he had faced and overcome, not bitter.

A young man, the driver, got out of the car. And then the other door opened, and a young woman climbed out. She reached into the back seat and retrieved a baby!

It was obvious the young woman had had a terrible fright, and Noelle got out of the vehicle and went to her. She held out her arms to the baby, and found it snuggled against her.

They went and sat in Aidan's warm vehicle while the two men figured it out. Aidan had a towrope in their vehicle, and he soon had the blue car back on the road. They determined it was safe to drive and the little family was back on their way.

Noelle sighed contentedly, as they too got back on their way. "Did that feel like the perfect Christmas moment to you?"

Aidan cocked his head and squinted, thinking about it.

And then he turned to her, and gave her perhaps the most radiant smile she had ever seen.

"Perfect," he agreed.

Again the storm deepened around them. When they turned off the secondary highway to the country lane that eventually would lead to Rufus's ranch, there had been no plows. The snow was unbelievably deep and the going was slow. Still, there was that feeling of being in a capsule with him, warm and safe, a wonderful intimacy blossoming between them.

Normally the drive from Calgary to her grandfather's took a little over two hours. They had been on the road for eight when they finally turned at the wooden gate that marked the beginning of his road. The last light was leeching from the short winter day. They were less than six kilometers from Christmas! From lights and egg nog and singing around the tree, from Tess's excitement and wonder, from a fire in the living room stone fireplace that was lit only once or twice every year.

Her grandfather had obviously been out on the tractor, clearing the road. His road appeared to be in better shape than the lane had been.

But then, without warning, a huge snow-laden tree crashed across the road in front of them. The sudden cloud of snow that enveloped them was dramatic and oddly silent.

Aidan stomped on the brakes and the big sturdy vehicle shuddered to a halt, its windshield wipers clearing away the sudden onslaught of yet more snow, the bumper practically resting on the branches of the fallen tree.

Aidan leaned back, closed his eyes, and then turned and looked at her. "A few seconds later..."

"I know." Her heart was thudding crazily.

They both let that sink in. That life could change that quickly in a few seconds.

After getting over the initial shock, she reached for her phone.

"I'll just call Grandpa. He'll come for us in the tractor."

She glared at her phone.

"Let me guess," Aidan said quietly. "We're already in the twilight zone of no service."

"He's going to be so worried. Should we walk?"

Aidan squinted out into the snow. "No, I don't think so. It's getting dark, the storm is making visibility really poor. The road is going to disappear again fairly shortly. There are just too many stories of people getting lost in stuff like this. I'd rather sit tight until morning."

"My grandfather will be worried about us."

"You know, your grandfather strikes me as a guy who has dealt with a lot of stuff in his time. He's used to this country, to bad weather, and poor roads and nonexistent communication, and nature throwing a kink in the best-laid plans.

I think he'll be okay, and I think he'll make it okay for Tess and Nana."

And then something else sank in, at least for her.

That a person could do whatever they wanted, have any plan they wanted, but there were bigger forces to contend with.

Sometimes, no matter how badly you wanted to be home for Christmas, it just was not going to happen.

"What is that over there?"

Noelle followed his gaze. A shape was barely visible through the blowing, thick snow.

"Oh!" she said. "We're at the old honeymoon cabin."

He turned and gave her a look. "You're kidding, right?"

"No," she said. "I'm not kidding at all."

# CHAPTER FOURTEEN

NOELLE ACTUALLY FELT herself blushing under his incredulous gaze. It wasn't as if she had planned for them to happen upon the honeymoon cabin!

"A honeymoon cabin in the middle of nowhere," he said, his voice threaded through with disbelief.

"It's not really in the middle of nowhere," Noelle said. "All this land used to be McGregor land. My grandfather sold it this year. There's no one left to ranch it."

He reached out and squeezed her hand at the emotion in her voice.

"Anyway, we're quite close to the old property boundary. My great-great-great-grandfather built the first cabin right there to bring his new bride home. If legend is correct, he'd talked his old sweetheart into coming from Scotland to join him. Later, they built the bigger house in a place closer to water and more protected from the wind."

"Well, let's go see if it's habitable. It would probably be a more comfortable place to spend the night than the truck."

But when she got out of the truck, her weak ankle turned again. She tried to muffle her little cry of pain, but Aidan, who had gone ahead, came back immediately. "Wait here a sec. I'll go see if it's locked."

"No one around here would lock a cabin. For the very reason we find ourselves in now. Somebody might need it."

"In that case…"

He swooped her up in his arms and plowed through the snow, holding her tight to his chest. He made her feel light as a feather, protected, cared for.

He went up the snow-clogged steps, managed to wrestle the door handle open while juggling her in his arms, and then—

"Don't!" she said.

But it was too late. He had carried her over the threshold of the Honeymoon Cabin.

She giggled and buried her head in his shoulder. It was too easy to imagine being carried over this threshold by him in different circumstances.

He gave her a wry look, and then set her down at a chair at the sturdy table by the woodstove. He went back to the vehicle and retrieved the emergency kit, which had a flashlight in it. He shone the beam around.

Noelle hugged herself against the deep chill permeating the cabin. Despite the cold in the room a certain warmth shone through.

It was just one simple room, but it was lovely. She was surprised to see the red plaid curtains over the one window looked new. They were so homey. There was a matching tablecloth on the table. She lifted a corner. Hand-sewn.

A large, colorful rag rug, the kind her grandmother had made, covered the main area, but she had never seen one quite this large before.

Over in one corner was a bed hewn from logs, the mattress and bedding rolled tight and wrapped in plastic against invading rodents.

In the opposite corner was the kitchen—a few shelves with crockery and pots and pans, a counter, an old enamel bowl.

"It became a tradition," Noelle said slowly. "Everyone had their honeymoon here. My parents were probably the last ones."

She looked again at the new window coverings and at the tablecloth. She stared at the rug. She noticed, even in the dark, that there were framed embroideries on the walls.

It wasn't even on her grandparents' land anymore, but somehow she knew. Her grandmother, thinking Noelle was going to marry Mitchell, had asked to use it, and had gotten it ready for them. It had probably been one of the last things she'd done.

Noelle began to cry. Aidan came and put his arms around her, held her tight.

"Hey," he said. "It's okay. It's been a long day."

"A long, good day," she said, forcing her voice past the tightness in her throat. "I was crying because I think my Grandma McGregor got this ready for me, before she died. For my honeymoon."

"If I ever find that guy," he promised fiercely, "I'm going to smack him right on his sunburned bald head."

She hiccupped through tears and laughter. "No, don't do that. I'm not sorry I'm not marrying Mitchell. Not anymore."

She contemplated that for a second. When *exactly* had she begun to understand it was a blessing that he had gone? When had she begun to see that, in settling for an imitation, she could have missed the real thing?

For the first time, she felt forgiveness for Mitchell. Something in him had *known* it wasn't quite right.

It was still lousy that he had cleared the bank account, but in retrospect, it had been a small price to pay for an extremely valuable lesson.

"I'm beginning to see that it was not going to be right for me. They're not sad tears," she finally managed to hiccup. "I just, for a moment there, felt so close to them. I can feel their love in the room."

"I can feel it, too," he said softly, coming and standing behind her, draping himself over her chair to hold her.

She reared her head back to look at him. "What? You can? Aidan Phillips? Mr. Cynic?"

"Maybe it's a Christmas thing," he said, smiling. "Okay, let's get some heat happening."

He let her go and went to investigate the wood heater. "There's kindling," he said, surprised. "And some wood, enough to get us started, anyway."

"These cabins are always left ready to use. You just never know when a stranger might need shelter."

He turned and looked at her. "It's kind of like finding a manger, isn't it?"

The skeptic in him seemed to be completely gone. Gone since he had shared his secrets last night. "Yes," she whispered. "It is."

They were silent, both of them feeling the sacredness, a connection to each other and to a shared moment of finding shelter in an unexpected place on a night when it was so needed.

Aidan got the fire started, and soon the

flames were crackling. The heat in the small space was instant.

"Don't look so surprised," he said. "I was a Boy Scout, you know."

That must be where he had learned the value of good deeds! He went back into the storm and soon was back in the cabin, arms laden with supplies from the vehicle.

Then Aidan found an ax and went outside. While she listened to the steady rhythm of him chopping wood, Noelle got up from the chair and limped around the small space. She found oil for the lamps and lit them. She looked through the cupboards. Tinned goods were never left, because they could freeze and explode. A mouse had been in the boxed soups and biscuit mix.

"Aidan?" She limped out to the porch. There was already wood stacked neatly there. What was he doing? Over the ferocious howl of the wind, she could hear him chopping away in the darkness.

He must not have seen the wood stacked on the porch. Despite being a Boy Scout, he was a city guy—he wouldn't know you couldn't burn a freshly cut tree.

Favoring her leg with the twisted ankle, Noelle went into the storm herself, filling several buckets with snow. Then she began the task of melting it into water on the stove. While that was happening, she got the mattress out of the wrapping and made the bed. It was a lovely feeling, making the cabin homey for Christmas Eve.

Still. One bed. Again. She was not sure tonight would end the same as last night had. Noelle was not at all sure she could any longer keep from loving him in every sense of that word. She ached for him. She ached for the taste of his lips and the feel of his hands, and for the steadiness of his eyes on her. She ached for a completeness between them.

She heard him on the porch.

The door flew open, and Noelle saw that Aidan had not been chopping firewood in the forest. Not at all.

He had found them the perfect Christmas tree and he wrestled it in the door, leaving puddles of snow as he crossed the floor.

"For you," he said. He dropped the tree and went back to shut the door against the storm screaming in through it.

Noelle was glad he had turned his back for a moment. She had to compose herself. Somehow, Aidan going out into the storm to get this tree, for her, meant more than the necklace she still wore around her neck.

Aidan went back to the tree. Because of the unevenness of how the trunk had been cut, standing it up proved a near impossible task, but created waves of laughter between the two of them. As they contemplated their options, together, Noelle could feel the bonds deepening between them.

Finally, with one of the tree's branches nailed to the wall to keep it from falling over, it was ready for decorations. They made decorations out of anything they could find. There was a ball of string on one of the lower kitchen shelves and so they strung pine cones they found close to the cabin. They made snowballs out of napkins and garlands out of toilet tissue. They cut angels and snowmen and stars from a stack of bright green paper plates they found.

When they couldn't fit one more thing on their beautiful tree, they pulled the table close and sat down admiring it. They drank hot chocolate and ate all her stocking stuffers for supper.

On one of the shelves they found a deck of cards, and he showed her how to play some poker hands. And then she showed him how to play Ninety-Nine. And then, in honor of Tess, they played Go Fish and Crazy Eights.

It was the best Christmas Eve she had ever had. As the wind shrieked outside and snow pelted the windows, here inside the cabin there was a richness in the air itself. It was cozy. There were no distractions, no cell phone service, no need to "check" the constant incoming media. There was no TV and no computers. There was simplicity. Warmth. Food. Each other.

They laughed until they hurt as they played the card games, and made up new rules, and said silly things, and playfully cheated, and made up excuses to touch each other's hands.

But then the laughter died.

And was replaced by something else when his hand lingered on hers just a little too long. Their eyes met and held. A sizzling awareness leaped up between them, like embers that had smoldered harmlessly and suddenly burst into flame.

Noelle could barely breathe as desire chased every other thing from her mind: every worry, every past heartache, every thought for the future, gone. Obliterated in the need to strengthen the connection between them.

He put pressure on her hand, increasing it until she followed its command, out of her own chair and onto his lap. She raked his beautiful hair with her hands, loving the silken feel of it. He touched the tendrils of hers with a certain gentle reverence.

But then the gentleness—if not the reverence— was gone. Replaced by heat. And hunger.

He placed his hand on the back of her neck and pulled her mouth to his.

Sweet, sweet welcome. At first, it was tenderness and joyous exploration. It was taste and scent and sensory overload. When it felt as if she might explode for the sensation, it intensified again, becoming something more, more urgent, more compelling, uncontrollable and unstoppable.

A command as ancient as time.

Noelle felt a primal need burning within her, to know him in every way it was possible for a woman to know a man. The Christmas cottage faded. The tree and the warm glow of the oil lamps disappeared from her consciousness. All that existed in her world was Aidan.

Aidan and his chocolate-flavored kisses. Aidan and his deep blue eyes. Aidan and the scrape of his whiskers across her sensitive skin. Aidan and the fresh-cut pine smell that clung to him. Aidan and the way his hands felt as they brailled her face and her earlobes and her neck and the dip between her breasts.

Her hands went under his shirt and touched his naked flesh. His skin was molten and silky. His muscles were enticingly hard beneath her fingertips.

He stood up from the chair, with her in his arms, and carried her to the bed. He set her down on it with exquisite tenderness, and then he stood staring at her, the brightness of his eyes clouded with desire. She held out her arms to him, and with a groan of pure surrender, he came down, lowering himself on top of her.

She felt the full length of him, his sinewy strength. She shuddered with wanting.

He plundered her then with his tongue. He plundered the insides of her ears and the hollow of her collarbone. He ran his tongue down the length of her neck and lower.

And then his lips found hers again.

And all innocence was lost.

This was a man. Pure, 100 percent, unadulterated man. He was a warrior. And a prince. He was unleashed, barely tamed. He was a man who knew what he wanted.

She welcomed this side of him.

She welcomed him to lose his legendary control. She reveled in the fact that she was the one who had made it happen. But just as she felt victory close, he pulled away from her. Panting, he sat on the edge of the bed.

"I can't," he said.

"Yes, you can," she whispered, her voice raw with need.

"No, I can't."

"Why?" she asked devastated. "Why?"

Why? Aidan looked at her beautiful face, flushed with longing. For *him*. But it was wrong on so many levels.

She did not even know this about herself, but Noelle McGregor was not this kind of woman. At all. She was the kind of woman that asked more of a man. Demanded more of a man. That a man with any moral fiber at all had to ask himself very hard questions before he took it to the next level.

She'd already been with one man who was completely unworthy of her. Who had not asked the hard questions.

Where was it going? What could he offer? Did he have honorable intentions for the future?

Aidan had to look at this realistically. They had known each other days, not weeks, not months. It seemed impossible to feel this strongly about her, to have her feel this strongly about him. Was the intensity of this experience, of being snowbound together in this little cabin, creating illusions that could not stand up to the test of reality?

And yet, when he looked at her, that word, *forever*, seemed for the first time in a long time like something he could actually hope for.

And if he was prepared to offer forever, in what way was it honorable to do this first? She was a woman who deserved a slow courtship. Who deserved to be cherished and honored and respected. Who deserved *I do*.

And before that, even, who deserved to be

buried under gifts that caused her wonder. She deserved to be courted: to be taken dancing. And for candlelit dinners. And for long walks. And on journeys of delight.

Perhaps it was being a single dad to a daughter that made him so aware of the right way to do things. He wanted to give Noelle everything he hoped a worthy suitor would someday give Tess.

When he looked into her face, Aidan knew he'd been given the best Christmas gift of all. The one he had always hoped for and had come, over time, not to believe in.

He had fallen in love with Noelle McGregor. Or it felt as if he had.

But if it was true, it needed to survive the intensity of what they had experienced over the last few days.

He could not hold out that hope to her until he was 100 percent certain it was true.

"What?" she whispered, reading every thought that crossed his face with consternation.

"Merry Christmas," he said to her softly, giving her the best present he knew. Honoring her.

He moved away from her slowly. He knew he dared not look back at her, lying on that bed, her eyes imploring him. Aidan put on his jacket and his boots. He opened the door to the scream of the wind and the relentless pelting of snow.

The best thing for both of them would be if it cooled down between them, if they made no decisions while in this fever of wanting.

"I'm going to sleep in the truck," he told her.

Walking away from her willingness was just about the hardest thing Aidan Phillips had ever done.

# CHAPTER FIFTEEN

*CHRISTMAS.* AIDAN WAS astounded that that was his first thought. His neck hurt from sleeping in the truck, and he was cold. He had turned the engine on and off through the night, but it was currently off.

Then he knew why it had been his first thought.

Impossibly, he could hear the sharp jangle of bells. He sat up on the seat and peered out the windshield, but it was covered in a thick layer of snow. The sound of bells grew louder, and then a little girl's laugh.

Aidan tumbled out of the truck. The sun had come out and nearly blinded him with its brilliance, the fresh, deep snow sparkling with a million blue lights.

A horse-drawn sleigh was coming toward him, huge gray horses throwing up clouds of snow, a sleigh skimming along behind them.

And in that sleigh was Rufus and Nana and Tess, Smiley packed onto the front seat with them.

The sleigh pulled up beside him, the huge horses blowing warm steam out their noses. Tess, radiant, held out her arms and he picked her off the seat, kissed her cheek, held her close.

"Merry Christmas, Daddy!"

"Merry Christmas, Tess."

He scanned her face. If she had experienced a moment's concern about her father not arriving for Christmas Eve, it did not show in her sparkling eyes now.

"Guess what?" Tess breathed. "Santa didn't come. Rufus said it's the first time, ever, that a snowstorm has stopped Santa." Tess sighed with contentment, somehow thrilled to have been a part of this historic event.

Aidan sought Rufus's eyes over Tess's shoulder, thanking him for managing to twist it in such a way that it deepened the magic for Tess instead of destroying it.

"Santa will come tomorrow, instead," Tess said officiously. "He will need extra cookies and the reindeer will need extra carrots."

A Christmas disaster transformed. A little girl thinking not of her own disappointment but of poor Santa's discomfort.

"We didn't open any presents," Tess said.

"Why not?" Aidan asked her, ruffling her hair.

"Daddy! Silly! It's not Christmas without you."

He looked into her sparkling eyes and felt

deep gratitude for the amazing gift of his little girl. He felt the love between them that he had so often witnessed between Noelle and her grandfather. He felt grateful that, despite all his doubts about his parenting abilities, despite his bumbling, Tess seemed to be turning out just fine.

"How did you find us?" Aidan asked Rufus.

Rufus looked...different. And so did Nana. They both looked younger, brimming over with *something* that had nothing to do with the crisp morning sleigh ride.

"I figured you'd get as far as the lane. A tree fell outside the house last night, too. Wiped out the power. And then I just kind of went *Ah, I bet they're at the cabin.* Where's Noelle? How come you're in the truck when there's a perfectly good cabin right there?"

Aidan shuffled uncomfortably and Rufus gave a snort of knowing laughter.

"Protecting my granddaughter's virtue, were you?" And then softly, and with utter sincerity, "Good man."

For some reason, the older man's approval and praise meant a great deal to him. It made the sacrifice he had made last night worth it. Aidan met his eyes with a sheepish smile.

And then the door of the cabin opened and Noelle came out.

Aidan watched her and felt his heart swell.

She was beautiful. With no makeup and her hair flying every which way, and her crumpled clothes from yesterday, she was beautiful. As beautiful as she had been in that extraordinary red dress. He had done the right thing. There was no way he could have shared a bed with her two nights in a row with nothing happening.

She started to come toward them smiling, an endearing shyness in her smile, just a hint of uncertainty as her eyes met his and then skittered away.

Aidan noticed she was still limping ever so slightly, and he went to her. She gazed up at him, asking, imploring. He smiled reassuringly, touched her cheek. "Happy Birthday," he said softly.

"Merry Christmas, Aidan."

"Happy Birthday, my little Christmas star!" Rufus got down off the sleigh with a vigor that belied his age. He went to Noelle and picked her up and swung her around. She laughed out loud and kissed her grandfather's weathered cheek.

Aidan felt it right then. Something stinging behind his eyes as he watched them. He felt the longing he had been outrunning since he was a little boy.

It was in the very air between Noelle and her grandfather. The love. The sense of family. The deep knowing that they would always have a place to come home to.

Could he have that, too? What a gift it would be to give his daughter such a thing. It would require the bravest thing of all: to hope again, to say yes.

Greetings dispensed with, Rufus went and surveyed the tree that had fallen in front of the truck.

"Should be able to move that with the tractor. I had to cancel, though, Old-fashioned Country Christmas. I didn't want anyone risking life and limb to get here. Plus, there's no power. Pretty hard to cook a turkey dinner without that. Good thing I still have that old rotary phone that you young people think is so funny. You don't need power to make a few calls. And we got the woodstove. You can cook a few rudimentary things on that."

"Aw, Grandpa," Noelle said. "I'm sorry about your Christmas plans."

"Ha." Rufus lifted a shoulder. "You get to be my age and you figure it all out—there's a greater plan. It's probably better than anything I could ever plan for myself, anyway."

Those words seemed to fill every space in Aidan's head as they began loading gifts out of the truck and into the sleigh. Tess wanted to sit in the front with Nana and Rufus, and Aidan found himself under a shared blanket with No-elle. He took her hand and squeezed it gently.

He thought of the strange set of events that had brought them together. He thought of playing in the snow with her, and her eyes on him as he had cut down the tree. He thought of her laughing as he bungled gingerbread decorating. He thought of them sitting in the cold in the hayloft looking at stars. He thought of the new lightness in her spirit as she had owned that red dress and owned the Enchantment Ball. He thought of how he'd confided his broken dreams to her and how it had felt—not like a weakness, but like an invitation to wake up, to live again. He thought of driving with her through the storm, and her incredible calm and bravery. He thought of decorating that funny little tree with her last night, and playing cards, and laughing until his stomach hurt.

It seemed as if it could be true. All part of a greater plan.

Noelle gave him her full attention, scanning his face. And whatever she found there reassured her, because she broke out in a smile.

Aidan felt himself reach for what he saw in Noelle's eyes. He watched his daughter wrap her arms around the dog as the sleigh lurched forward, and he saw Nana slip her arm around

Rufus's waist. He saw the old man's smile as he turned his head to look at Nana.

Love. It was in the air. Was it possible that was what was really part of a greater plan? It all boiled down to that, didn't it? That simple instruction, the one the seed had been planted for on a Christmas Day a long, long time ago.

Love one another.

Love the strangers you met along the way. And the family you'd been given, even with their flaws.

Love one another.

Every single time that magnificent force— love—came to you, say *yes* instead of no.

Aidan felt that question intensify within himself. Could he say yes to what he had waited his entire life to feel?

A sense of being part of something larger than himself?

He struggled for a moment. It seemed overwhelming. The cynic in him tried to rise up, one last time. But then he felt even that part of him surrender to it, that larger force, which sparkled in the air on this snowy Christmas morning.

Inwardly, he heard a whisper. Yes. And then louder, a celebration, yes.

Noelle felt his surrender. She had not been aware that some heaviness remained in Aidan, until it was gone, until she saw a new sparkle in his eyes when he looked at her.

Her grandfather wheeled the horses around and they headed back across the fluffy banks of sparkling snow, toward the distant home place. The horses' manes lifted, and their footsteps beat a muffled tattoo in the snow. Their bells could have been church bells; they rang across the crisp air with such purity.

"Gee up," her grandfather said, slapping the reins. The horses changed gait easily, pulling forward powerfully, the sleigh skimming along behind them. Tess laughed out loud, and, if Noelle was not mistaken, Nana tucked herself against Rufus just a little more tightly. It was cold, and yet the sun, the blanket and most especially Aidan's hand in hers made it seem bright and warm.

It was Aidan's voice that lifted in song. "Jingle bells, jingle bells, jingle all the way…"

His voice was beautiful, strong and steady, a pure tenor. Tess clapped her pink-mittened hands with delight and looked at her father's face with pure wonder, the wonder of a child who still believed in the magic and the miracles of Christmas.

Her voice, innocent and bold, joined her father's. And then they were all singing, and the dog was howling along, and it was, possibly, the best Christmas moment Noelle had ever experienced. When that song died, another one rose to take its place. They sang all the way back to the house.

While Rufus looked after the horses, Nana herded them all inside and managed to do quite nicely, putting together a Christmas breakfast on the woodstove.

After they had eaten, Tess was not waiting one more second for her presents. Aidan managed to spirit Jerry Juicejar away for delivery by Santa the next day, but aside from that, the living room was soon filled with torn wrapping paper and her squeals of delight.

Tess presented Noelle with a gift. She was being unusually shy.

"I didn't have anything for you, so I made it."

Noelle unwrapped her gift to find a carefully illustrated and printed book. It was a story about a girl whose birthday fell on Christmas. "This is amazing. I can't believe you could make such a thing. You're only five."

"Nearly six," Tess said, beaming nonetheless. "Nana had to help me with some of it."

Noelle stared at the painstaking printing and knew she would cherish the handmade book forever.

The skates were the biggest hit, and Tess insisted they must go to the pond immediately.

They all piled outside, skates strung over their shoulders. The pond was covered in nearly a foot of snow, so after testing the thickness of the ice, Rufus fired up the tractor and cleared the whole thing. After that, he invited Nana up into the crowded cab with him, and they headed off to clear the road and move the tree. He waved off Aidan's offer of help.

Noelle watched, delighted, as Aidan coached Tess through her first time on skates. She had seen glimpses of it all along, but he seemed newly relaxed, some guard completely down, and it was heart-warming to see what a good dad he was, patient, firm, funny.

Nana and Rufus returned, Nana driving Aidan's vehicle back down the cleared road. And then the elderly couple put on skates, too. They took over Tess's coaching, and the beautiful little girl skated off between Rufus and Nana, holding both their hands.

And then Aidan held out his hand to Noelle. And they skated until their legs hurt and laughed until they could laugh no more. He hummed "Could I Have This Dance," and they tried dancing together on skates, ending up in a tangled heap, Noelle beneath him, looking up into his sapphire eyes with wonder.

*Could this really be happening to her?*

It was Christmas Day and it was her birthday and she was in love, and it was the best day she had ever had. But in the back of her mind she heard a whisper, *Tomorrow is Boxing Day.* She shoved the thought away. Surely, everything had changed...

When exhaustion and cold finally set in, a huge bonfire was lit and a kettle of hot chocolate placed beside it. They roasted wieners for Christmas lunch, and then, when the power did not come back on, again for dinner.

"The best Christmas ever," Tess mumbled, with little smudges of mustard and ketchup smeared around the bow of her mouth.

"Yes," Aidan agreed, his eyes meeting Noelle's. "The best Christmas ever."

"And Santa is still going to come tomorrow, isn't he? I have to put out cookies. I have to put out—"

But Tess fell asleep in her father's arms before these important errands could be completed. The bonfire light was casting her face in gold and Aidan's, too, and the stars winked on in an ink-dark sky. They finally retreated to the house, Tess nestled into Aidan's shoulder.

Aidan and Noelle put the sleepy girl in her pajamas and tucked her into her bed together. She didn't even wake up. By the time they were done, Rufus and Nana had also disappeared. So the two of them put out milk and cookies for Santa, and retrieved Jerry Juicejar from his hiding place and put him under the tree. Then they hung the socks, one for each member of the household, and filled them with what was left of the Christmas treats.

They were small things. And yet they filled Noelle's heart with a sense of how it would be to be together, as a couple, as a family, as a mom and dad to Tess.

Was that where all this was going? When she looked into his eyes, her breath nearly stopped for the truth she saw there.

She touched his cheek.

He touched hers.

And the words found their way to her mouth.

"I love you."

She stood on her tiptoes and took his mouth.

"Hey," he protested, though the protest was weak, "there's no mistletoe."

She felt disappointed. Once again, he was the one backing away. Did it mean he did not feel the same way? Had she embarrassed herself? Was it ridiculous to make such a declaration after such a short time?

He stood there, utterly still, looking at her.

And then he spoke the words.

"I love you, too."

His voice was gruff with emotion. The words seemed to stun him. His moved his hand away from her cheek and stroked it over the swollen plumpness of her lip. Her tongue reached out and touched it, and he gasped with longing, but swiftly took his hand away. He looked at it, and then at her.

He wheeled away from her, and she heard his soft tread on the stairs, and then moments later, she heard his bedroom door softly, but firmly, close.

"The best Christmas ever," Noelle whispered, hugging herself tightly.

# CHAPTER SIXTEEN

"NOELLE, WAKE UP! Wake up." Tess was shaking her urgently. "We have to go downstairs and see if Santa came."

She opened her eyes slowly, loving this moment, and loving this little girl, loving the man who stood in the doorway of her room.

"I'm awake," she said. "Go get Nana and Rufus."

"They're up already. Come on. Come on."

Noelle got out of bed, self-conscious in the penguin jammies. She quickly put her housecoat on over the top, and followed Tess and Aidan down the stairs.

Tess stopped at the door of the living room. She shrieked and ran in. "It's Jerry!"

Noelle and Aidan came in behind her. Nana was in the room, but not Rufus. Noelle felt a moment's regret that her grandfather had missed this delightful moment.

But then Aidan put his hand around her shoulder and they exchanged a smile, bathed in the little girl's joy. Aidan kissed Noelle casually, on the mouth.

At that exact moment, Tess turned from Jerry. Her eyes went wide.

"Daddy?" she asked softly. "Is Noelle going to be my mommy?"

Aidan felt himself go still. He felt the shock of Tess's question wash over him. This was how poor a parent he had been. It was beyond bumbling. He'd been thinking of himself. He'd immersed himself in the joy of Noelle loving him.

He'd allowed himself to believe in miracles.

But he, of all people, should know better than that. What, in his world, in his experience, had given him the skill to make a relationship work? Hadn't he thought, once, filled with hope and dreams, that he could write his own story? That he could learn? That he could overcome the lack of love in his childhood?

His marriage had proved him so wrong. One thing about being good at business? You knew never to repeat the same mistake twice.

And not just for him. How could he drag his daughter down this road? How could he hold out to her a shining promise of a family? A mommy? Only to have her in the front row to view his failings when it all began to fall apart? Hadn't Tess been damaged enough?

And what of Noelle?

Could he do that to her? Could he take that offering of her sweet love and watch it turn to dust and ash? Could he be the one who put out the light he had seen in her eyes this morning when she had told him she loved him?

Had he really answered her? Had he really given her false hope? Had he really allowed temporary good feelings to sway his judgment for the future?

As a businessman he knew you could not do that. You had to rely on instincts, yes, but then you had to do the hard work, the research, the plausibility studies to back up those instincts. Just jumping in on a hunch, basing your move on a feeling, was catastrophic in business.

The plausibility study, he realized, had already been done. He had not passed the litmus test with Sierra. He could not drag his daughter through another failure.

As a shocked stillness came over the room, Aidan moved a step away from Noelle. She looked as if she was holding her breath, waiting to hear how he would respond to that innocent question.

But he was saved from answering.

"What?" Nana was at the window, and she

had looked out, possibly to give the couple at least an illusion of privacy as they contemplated the enormity of the question that had just been asked. "What has that old fool gone and done now?"

Aidan, looking for respite from the awkwardness of the question, went and stood at the window beside Nana.

He felt his heart break in two. Rufus was shuffling across the yard with a pony. There was a red ribbon around its neck.

It wasn't just Tess. And Noelle. It was Rufus, too. And Nana. All hoping for love to win.

Maybe Rufus had been matchmaking from the start. Maybe he'd gotten a pony for Tess in the hope of keeping all their lives tangled together once Christmas was over. The old guy probably knew any man with a brain was going to fall in love with Noelle given time and the right circumstances. Rufus, with that pony, was setting things up so that nature could take its course.

Aidan felt a crushing responsibility to stop this train before it got too out of control, before it caused a wreck that took everyone down with it.

"Did you know about this?" he asked Noelle. The heartbreak had been stripped from his voice, and in its place was the pure ice of a man who knew he had to be cold enough to save everyone around him who was foolish enough to give him one more chance to get it right.

Noelle joined him at the window. Here came Rufus and Smiley through the snow, leading Gidget, who had a bow around her neck. It did not look like the little horse had cooperated with the bow-tying exercise, as it was hanging crookedly.

Noelle scanned Aidan's face. He looked so very cold, his beloved features cast in stone. She didn't want to admit she'd known, but she couldn't just throw her grandfather under the bus, either.

She nodded, and something hardened in Aidan's face.

"Please keep Tess away from the window," Aidan said tersely. And then without even putting on a jacket he slipped into shoes by the door and went out into the cold.

Noelle could not bear to watch what happened. She got down on the floor with Tess, who was busy taking Jerry out of his wrapper and exploring the Juicejar house.

It seemed like a long time later that Aidan came back, followed by her grandfather, who gave her a baffled look and lifted his shoulder. Neither man said anything about the pony.

"Time for us to pack our bags," Aidan said, knocking the snow off his boots, refusing to look at Noelle.

So, he was on his original schedule, after all.

"I'm not leaving!" Tess screamed. "I'm not leaving Smiley. I'm not leaving Noelle and Rufus. We're building a snowman today. We're making cookies. We're—" her voice dissolved into a sob.

Noelle went and gathered the little girl in her arms. What could she say? She could not make her any promises. When she glanced at Aidan's face, she did not see any hope for a future there. How had it all fallen apart so quickly?

But for now, it was not her heartbreak she needed to focus on. It was Tess. "It's all right, sweetheart," she whispered to the little girl, feeling her chest get wet with tears. She stroked her hair. "Everything will be all right," she said. As she glanced again at Aidan, it didn't feel that way. It felt like nothing could ever be right again.

"Can I see you outside?" Aidan asked Noelle. The coldness in his tone chilled her to the bone.

Noelle, with a final kiss on Tess's silky hair, put the little girl away from her. "Go gather up your things," she said softly.

She put on her coat and went outside. He already had his vehicle warming up. She hugged herself, quite a different hug than the one last night.

"What happened?" she asked, scanning his features so closed to her.

"I've had a wonderful time," he said formally. "As has Tess. I can't thank you enough for the Christmas you have given my daughter and myself."

Who was this cool stranger?

"I won't be seeing you again, Noelle."

Even though she had already sensed it, this announcement was like being hit with a pail of cold water. Her mouth fell open. Her voice was trembling. "W-w-what? W-w-why?"

"I can't do it to Tess," he said softly. "I can't hold out all this hope to her, and then watch her world come tumbling down around her again."

"Does it have to? Come tumbling down?"

"I trusted you. I told you the only rule for Christmas was no pony, and you knew. Can you see how that would have forced us to keep coming back here? Forced us to tangle our lives more and more with yours? And your grandfather's? It was extremely manipulative."

"You pompous ass! My grandfather was trying to make a little girl happy. How dare you make that about you? How dare you make those judgments of him when he has been nothing but generous to you? That speaks to you. Not to him."

"Yes," Aidan said sadly. "It does. It speaks to me. Goodbye, Noelle."

She stood there quivering with fury and shock. She would not give him the satisfaction of crying in front of him. She whirled and went back in the house.

She hugged Tess and Nana, who were both coming down the stairs with their packed things, looking shocked.

And then, as quickly as their guests had come, they were gone, and Noelle was there alone with her grandfather.

"I'm sorry," he said. "I didn't think through the pony thing."

"Oh, Grandpa," Noelle said, and went and put a reassuring arm around his shoulders. "You have the best heart of any man I know. Don't ever doubt that."

"Why did they leave then?" her grandfather asked grumpily.

She thought of Tess's innocent question, and she thought of that word poking out from under the Christmas wreath on the front door. Hope.

"It has to do with the most dangerous thing of all," she said softly.

"Ah," Rufus said. "Love. He'll come around."

But Noelle thought of the stony look on Aidan's face, and somehow she doubted that he would, even as she nursed the most dangerous thing of all.

Hope.

For some reason, Noelle finally remembered what her grandmother had said, that night she had overheard her grandparents talking during her and Mitchell's visit to the ranch.

*What's wrong with him?* her grandfather had asked of Mitchell.

For the longest time, Noelle had not remembered her grandmother's answer. But now she did, so clearly she wondered how she could have ever thought she'd forgotten.

*It's not what's wrong with him,* her grandmother had said. *It's what's wrong with her to accept that kind of treatment.*

That was why it had flitted around the edges of her mind, like a wily cat that did not want to be caught. Because she could not bear it that her beloved grandmother had thought there was something wrong with her.

Now, the entire conversation came pouring back.

*She longs to be loved,* Rufus had said. *He doesn't deserve that.*

And her grandmother had said, *You don't choose a man like that if you long to be loved. I think you choose a man like that if you are*

*scared to death of being loved. It has already
hurt you so badly, you can't do it again.*

Right there, on Boxing Day, Noelle stood in
the wisdom and light and truth of her grandmother's words. She had chosen Mitchell because he would require less of her heart, not
more.

She was aware she was not that woman anymore.

Noelle was aware she had spent too much of
her life already waiting for a man to come to
his senses. She was done with that. She would
not demean herself in that way again.

She loved Aidan, but it occurred to her, after
she had left her grandfather's and gone back to
work, that love didn't weaken people. It made
them stronger.

And so she vowed to be stronger for loving
Aidan. She vowed not to be a woman scared to
death of being loved.

She refused to sit around eating ice cream
for supper and sulking. She fought the temptation to weep and wring her hands, and ask
what might have been. Instead, she decided to
become the woman in the red dress, to own
her own life.

She quit all her social media outlets. She did
not miss them. She didn't want to live vicari-
ously. She wanted to live! And so she became

a volunteer who read to children at the library. If it made her yearn for Tess, that was part of the price of loving. She took a ballroom dancing class, and loved that so much she signed up for a jazz class, too.

Still, every time the phone rang, she hoped.

Every time she saw a dark head moving through a crowd on a downtown street, she hoped.

Every time she heard "Could I Have This Dance," she hoped.

Because now she knew something she had not known before: that life could change in a second, that good things and miraculous things could come to you as quickly and as shockingly as loss.

One night, her phone rang as she was leaving her dance class, which had run quite late. Her grandfather would not call at this time of the night unless there was a problem. She answered the phone with a faint fear beating in her heart.

Silence.

And then a whisper. "Noelle?"

It was not her grandfather. The hair stood up on the back of her neck as she recognized that childish, sweet voice. "Tess?"

"We need you."

"What?"

"You said everything would be all right! You promised."

Noelle knew she had not promised, but she also knew the little girl had heard a promise, of sorts, and she felt the agony of missing them. "What's wrong, Tess?"

"My daddy was happy. He was happy when we were with you. I miss him being like that. I miss you." She started to cry. "He's so grumpy. He says he's not mad, but he acts like he is. He's on his phone all the time. I need you to come make my daddy happy again."

"Where are you?" Noelle asked, worried. Why was Tess whispering? Where was Aidan? She could not imagine he had allowed Tess to make this call.

"Daddy went in the shower so I took his phone. Because I hate his phone. I was going to hide it, but then I found your name. *N-o-e-l-l-e*."

Noelle tried to think why her number would be in his phone. Then, vaguely she recalled he had taken it when they were Christmas shopping, in case they lost track of each other in the busy mall.

"Did you remember I know my alphabet?"

"I remember everything about you, sweetheart."

"Before I hid it, I pushed your name. And you answered! I have the best hiding place for the phone. He'll never find it here. He won't even hear it ring. You want to guess?"

"The fridge?"

Tess laughed happily. "Farther away than that."

"Umm, the coat closet?"

"Nope, farther, even. You probably can't guess how far."

"You didn't go out of your apartment, did you?" Noelle asked, alarmed.

"I ran away," she said stubbornly.

"Are you in your apartment?"

Silence.

"Are you in the building?"

"Maybe," Tess said coyly.

"No one's with you? Where is Nana?"

"Nana's gone."

"Gone where?"

"To be with Rufus and Smiley."

Beneath her alarm, Noelle contemplated that. Not a word from her grandfather. How recent was this development?

"When did she go?" Noelle asked, trying to get some idea of how long Tess had been off on her adventure.

"I want to be with Rufus and Smiley, too."

"Are you by yourself right now, Tess?"

"Jerry is with me. I'm in a room with brooms. And shovels. It smells funny, but I don't care."

For a moment Noelle panicked. Jerry? Who was Jerry? Some creep who had found Tess and led her to the broom closet that smelled funny?

Oh! Jerry! Jerry Juicejar.

Noelle's mind raced. She could not hang up and call Aidan. She didn't even think she had Nana's number. Both must be frantic. Or did Nana even know? Did Aidan know? Or was he still in the shower?

"How long have you and Jerry been in the broom closet?" Not in their suite, Noelle deduced. They wouldn't need snow shovels in their suite. Tess was in the building. In some kind of janitorial room in the building.

"A long time," Tess said with a sigh. "I ate my chocolate candy already."

Noelle could tell Tess firmly to get out of the closet and go home. But the child was five! What if she took a wrong turn? Or met the wrong person?

Noelle oriented to where she was. She had walked to her dance class. She began to run toward Aidan's condo complex. Five minutes? Ten? She could not let Tess hear her panic.

Trying to keep the breathlessness out of her tone, she said, calmly and conversationally, "How is Jerry?"

"He's not as much fun as Smiley."

"Smiley misses you."

A little hiccupped sob. "I know. I miss him, too."

"Did I ever tell you about the dog I had when I was a little girl?"

"No." Reluctant curiosity.

"His name was Puddles."

"That's a good name!"

"Yes, it was, because at the beginning he made puddles all over the place. That's what puppies do."

Tess giggled.

"When he stopped making puddles, he got into other mischief. Once, when we were sleeping, he went into the bathroom and grabbed the end of the toilet paper roll in his teeth and ran all through the house with it. There was toilet paper everywhere."

Tess laughed. And Noelle kept talking. Five blocks.

"Once, my mom had made roast beef, and it was on the counter. She just left it for a minute, and when she came back in the room it was gone. And Puddles licked his lips and then he burped."

Four.

"Noelle! Dogs don't have lips."

"Don't they?"

"Smiley burped after he licked Nana's face."

Three.

"Yes, he did."

Two. She could see his condo complex. There

were police cars in front of it! Noelle put on a burst of speed, grateful for those jazz classes improving her lung capacity. She raced in the door.

Aidan was standing in the lobby in the middle of a knot of policeman. He was in his robe.

In a split second Noelle saw everything there was to see about him. She saw how deeply and completely he loved.

How deeply and completely he wanted to protect what he loved.

How deeply and completely he felt loss.

He saw her come in the doors. At first, it barely pierced his distress. But then, before his guard came up, she saw it.

The relief that she was here. The love—his love—that he had tried to protect her from, somehow seeing it as imperfect. Flawed. Doomed to failure.

She took the phone from her ear and pressed it to her chest, put a finger to her lips. The lobby went silent.

She went to him and stood on tiptoe.

"Maintenance room?" she whispered.

And he was racing down the hall with her behind him, and the police behind them both. He went down an emergency exit to the basement, raced down a dark hallway and threw open a door.

The ribbon of light that went in the door revealed Tess, Jerry pressed tight against chest, her mouth smeared with chocolate. She dropped the phone she had pressed to her ear.

Her father scooped her up and held her so tight it was a wonder the little girl could breathe.

"Daddy," Tess whispered, touching his cheek. "Are you crying?"

# CHAPTER SEVENTEEN

IT SEEMED IT was hours later that Tess was safely tucked into her own bed, ugly Jerry lodged comfortably beside her. The police were finally gone. Aidan sat on the sofa, his elbows on his knees, his head cradled in his hands.

Noelle brought him tea. He took it, and she sank down on the couch beside him.

His eyes met hers, the longing undisguised, before he looked quickly away. It was the face of a man tormented.

And Noelle knew why she had not allowed herself to sink into despair after his departure on the day after Christmas. She knew why, instead of taking to her bed and a bucket of ice cream, she had learned to dance and gone to read to children at the library.

Because love required her to find herself.

Love required her to be strong enough, sure enough in her own being, to go into the darkness he had wrapped himself in and bring him back out. To be brave enough to rescue this lonely, strong man who was determined to use his strength for all the wrong things. To keep love at bay, instead of to embrace it.

"I understand it now," she said softly. "You didn't leave because of a pony."

He was stubbornly silence.

"You used that as an excuse."

"What are you talking about?"

"I'm talking about you loving me."

He drew his breath in sharply. His mouth moved, but no sound came out. The fact that he seemed incapable of denying it gave her the courage to go on.

"You love me so much," Noelle told him softly, "that you thought you had to protect me. You couldn't possibly see yourself succeeding in this arena. How could you succeed at love?"

"Precisely," he said.

"You had no models for a good relationship. You saw that when you married Sierra. That you didn't have the tools to make it work."

He nodded.

"And yet your love for Tess is the model for all love," she told him softly.

"It's not. Look at what just happened. She ran away from me."

"Did she? Or did she know in her heart what

needed to happen? Did she sense somehow that you needed me?"

He looked as if he intended to protest. His mouth opened. But again, not a single sound came out.

"You were trying to protect both of us, Tess and me, weren't you, from what you saw as your inevitable failure?"

"Look, this conversation is pointless—"

"I agree," she said. "The time for talking is done."

He actually looked relieved. Until she leaned toward him. He could have gotten away, but he was paralyzed. She took his lips with her own. Tenderly. She let the touch of her lips tell him what he would not allow himself to hear in words.

That she was strong enough to face the storms.

That when his strength failed, hers would take over.

That she carried within her a legacy of such enormous love that the light of it would guide them both through the uncertain waters of a life together.

At first, his lips remained closed against hers. And yet, he did not push her away. She sensed he wanted to, but could not. And so she deepened her kiss until she felt the tiniest give in him, the tiniest of surrenders.

And into that gap, she poured everything she

was, and it was like sunlight pouring over snow, turning what was hard and cold into something silver and liquid.

He broke free of her lips, but he did not get up and leave. Or throw her out. Instead, he seemed to be eyeing the life rope she was throwing him.

"What if I hurt you?" Aidan whispered. "And in hurting you, hurt my daughter? She wants you as a mommy so desperately. I'm going to blow it."

"Are you?" Even though he had said that, she could see him reaching out for that rope.

"Yes," he said.

"Just trust it a little bit," Noelle told him. "Just trust love a little tiny bit, and see what it can do. Let's see what happens next."

For a long time, he said nothing. But then he took the rope she offered, Noelle saw the answer in his eyes, she saw in them that little flicker of light that was at the heart of the human spirit, and that was at the core of all human strength.

The ability, in the face of overwhelming evidence that it might be heartbreaking to do so, to still say yes to hope.

"All right," he said. "Let's see what happens next."

Over the next few months, Noelle discovered that Aidan was not a man who did anything by half measures, including seeing what happened next, including falling in love.

He courted her with an intensity, an attention to detail, a fierceness, a tenderness that made her feel as if she was the most loved woman in the world.

He wined her. He dined her. He showered her with gifts. They hiked the trails of Banff National Park and rode the gondola to the top of the world. They rode a different kind of gondola in Venice and snorkeled off the coast of Kona in Hawaii. They went to visit the wineries of the Sonoma Valley. They rode in a hot air balloon. They took a road trip and found each of the hidden hot springs of the Kootenays. They embraced adventures: rock climbing and kayaking and white water rafting. They took cooking classes and ballroom dancing classes.

They discovered what it meant for them to be a couple. Rufus and Nana, who had gotten married a scant two months after Christmas, happily took Tess when they went away.

And they discovered what it meant for them to be a family. They took Tess to Disney World in Florida, and the fabulous Atlantis resort in the Bahamas. They took in children's theaters and themed playgroups.

And for all this, Noelle's favorite moments with Aidan and Tess remained the simplest ones. Walking hand in hand along the Bow River as pussy willow buds burst in the trees. The three of them going together to story time at the library, or sprawled out on the floor of the children's section of the bookstore. Sitting on a bench and eating hotdogs at the truck downtown at lunch hour. All of them crowded into Tess's bed reading stories at night.

Best of all was when they went to the ranch together. Watching the quiet love grow between Nana and Rufus, and watching Tess learn to ride Gidget, playing board games at night and sitting in the hayloft together after everyone else had gone to bed.

The ranch was "their" place somehow, the place where, entirely free of distractions, something bolder and more beautiful than they had ever imagined for their lives had taken root.

They were at the ranch one summer evening when Aidan asked her to go for a walk with him.

They found themselves at the Honeymoon Cabin.

"I have a gift for you," he said quietly.

Noelle laughed. She had tried so hard to dissuade him from gifts, but there was no point. She took the envelope he held out to her. "What is it?"

"Open it."

Noelle opened it and found a sheaf of legal-looking papers.

"I don't understand what this is."

"Your grandfather took me aside a few weeks ago and gave me a talking-to."

"Really? What did he say?"

"He said he understood I was trying to do the honorable thing. He said he understood that it was important for a man to make the woman he loved feel as if she was a princess. He said he understood the value of an old-fashioned courtship. But he said enough was enough. He told me to get on with it."

Aidan was looking at her with a quiet intensity that made her heart stand still. That thing he did to her heart never seemed to change.

"He said time was shorter than a person could ever imagine. He said that's why he and Nana did things so quickly. Because they have both experienced losses and they have the maturity to understand that time runs out.

"He told me to marry you and have some babies, already."

"Aidan Phillips! Are you asking me to marry you?"

He was silent.

Even as her heart soared, Noelle could not resist teasing him. "Because my grandfather told you to?"

"Actually, he said all that after."

"After?"

"After I asked his permission. Quit rushing me!"

"His permission?"

"To marry his granddaughter."

Suddenly, Noelle didn't feel like teasing him anymore. This was real. This was what it all had been building toward: the time together, the increasingly heated looks and kisses. She loved spending time with him. She would not give up a moment of their romance.

But she was with her grandfather on this one.

She needed Aidan at a different level now. She needed to touch him in places where no one else touched him, and she needed to let the heat of his kisses spread until they were both weak with it. She needed there to be no more reasons to say no.

Aidan got down on one knee before her. She resisted the impulse to touch his hair.

He reached into his pocket and pulled out a velvet box. He snapped open the lid. The band within, studded with perfect diamonds, winked with astonishing blue lights. He cleared his throat.

"Noelle McGregor, I am so in love with you I can barely think for it. I am so in love with you I can barely breathe for it. You have taken a landscape that was bleak and dark and brought it to color and life. You have shown me the meaning of my life. You have become the role model for my daughter.

"I cannot imagine my life without you. I want to spend the rest of my days with you. I want to have children. I want to love you until you are breathless with my love.

"Will you marry me?"

Noelle was crying shamelessly. She dropped the papers he had given her and they scattered in the wind. She let her hands roam in his hair, relishing it, delighting in it. This incredible man was asking her to join lives with his. For the rest of their lives. Forever.

"Yes," she whispered. "Yes."

He rose to his feet and gathered her in his arms, and then shouted so loud the mountains sent an echo back to them.

"Thank you," he whispered. "Thank you for giving me something to hope for."

It was a long time before they came up for air.

"I guess we should find all those papers," he said reluctantly.

"What are they?"

"The deed for all this land. We're going to build our house here one day. And raise our children here."

"You bought back the McGregor land?"

"Every inch of it."

"But you're not a rancher!"

"I can learn. Plus, I figured you probably won't be able to keep your hands off me if I'm wearing a cowboy hat and riding a horse."

"I can barely keep my hands off you now," she said wryly.

"Oh, in that case, maybe I'll just lease the grazing rights."

It was her turn. "Thank you."

Not just for the land. In fact that seemed like the least of it. For all of it. For teaching her what love was. For giving her back her sense of family. For renewing her trust in life. For giving her a sense of herself, for allowing her to evolve into a woman worthy of love.

Worthy of him.

They turned, and hand in hand, they chased down all those papers that were scattering in the wind. It seemed those papers were playing with them, leading them on a path that pointed straight to the future.

# EPILOGUE

"I THINK WE should paint a hippopotamus on the wall," Tess said, her voice full of authority. At seven, she knew everything, including, apparently, what a new baby brother would require in his nursery.

"A hippopotamus?" Aidan repeated, trying to buy time. He wasn't quite sure that would fit with the nursery theme that he and Noelle had decided on—blue, jauntily nautical—to welcome their first child together, a boy, to the world. He didn't have a whole bunch of time for this, and a hippopotamus seemed like a rather large design change.

He gulped, trying not to think about the lack of time. In less than a week their baby was due.

"Maybe you should ask Mama," he suggested.

Tess had started calling Noelle Mama within a week of the wedding. Neither Noelle nor Aidan had suggested it; she had apparently come up with it on her own. Not Mommy, not a replacement for her mother who had died, but a new name.

"Ask me what?"

Aidan turned, paintbrush in hand, and looked at his wife.

She was exactly what he had recognized, what his heart had recognized—from the first moment she had thrown a snowball at him.

The most beautiful woman in the world. The woman who could change everything. The woman who was brave enough to come and rescue him from his lonely world.

"Can we have a hippopotamus in here?" Tess asked.

Noelle pretended to consider it. "Aren't they awfully big?" she asked, seriously. "Do you know what they eat?"

Tess's laughter, so frequent, so joyous, peeled through the room. "Painted on the wall, Mama. Not a real one."

Noelle contemplated the blank, pale blue wall. "I think that would be perfect," she said.

Aidan suppressed his groan.

Tess sighed with contentment, and went and cupped her hands on Noelle's tummy. "Hello, in there," she called loudly, "Hello, Ben."

And then she put her ear to Noelle's stomach. "I hear him," she decided. "Oh! He kicked me. Daddy! Come feel him."

And so he went and laid his hand over the tautness of Noelle's belly. Their eyes met as the baby seemed to do a somersault inside of her.

"Is it time?" he asked, stunned by the violent activity. "I'll get the car. I'll call Nana. I'll—"

Noelle was smiling at him, indulgently. She, and she alone, was entrusted with this truth. If he ran his billion-dollar company the way he awaited the birth of their baby—nervous, impulsive, jumping at every shadow—Wrangler would be broke.

Noelle, on the other hand, didn't seem the least bit worried about whether or not it was time. He had suggested they move back to his condo in the city until the baby arrived. When Noelle said no, he woke in the night, scanning the sky for storms. Even though it was fall—no chance of being snowed in, at all—he contemplated possible disasters. Trees falling. Water rising. Vehicles not starting.

Noelle had gotten up one night to find him coming in from outside.

"It's the middle of the night," she told him.

"I was just checking."

"Checking what?"

"It's windy."

She had cocked her head at him.

"A tree could come down over the driveway!"

"You could bring the helicopter out here," she

said. "A straight run to the hospital. Most of them even have landing pads right on the property."

He was actually thinking how brilliant she was, until he caught on that she was teasing him.

"A baby is nothing new here," she told him gently, when she saw the worry furrow his brow. You'd almost think she was planning on having it at home.

Home.

They had built the house last year, in a clearing not too far from the Honeymoon Cabin. He could actually see the old cabin from their master bedroom window upstairs.

They had, of course, had their honeymoon there. They'd married at the ranch just a few days before Christmas, a year to the day since they met.

Noelle could have had the wedding anywhere. She could have had a ball that would have matched the Christmas Enchantment Ball. She could have chosen a beach somewhere. She could have had a live band and dancing deep into the night.

Instead, they had exchanged their vows on the porch of the old ranch house. Tess had scattered snowflakes made out of paper instead of flower petals.

Noelle had said no to a white dress. She didn't

think it was the color of celebration. She thought it would just blend with all that snow.

Instead, she had looked gorgeous in a red gown, sure of herself, a woman confident enough to fly joyously in the face of tradition.

They could have had a feast catered by the best chef in Calgary. But Noelle had laughed that off. Instead, they had cleared the barn and plank tables had been set up that groaned under the weight of all the neighborhood women bringing their favorite dishes. After supper the tables had been cleared away, and the fiddles had come out. They had danced until dawn.

They could have had a honeymoon anywhere in the world. They could have left the ranch behind and flown to Tuscany, or to a private island a friend of his owned.

No. Instead, when the party was over, Rufus had hitched up the sleigh and delivered them to the Honeymoon Cabin.

They had spent five glorious days of exquisite time in that snowbound little cabin, with nothing but each other.

By then they had traveled much of the world together, witnessed marvels and discovered treasures beyond imagining.

And yet, in that cabin, there had been a sense of having everything they would ever need.

Each other.

He could not think of that time without his mouth going dry with wanting her. He could feel that desire build within him.

Not just to touch her, not just for the incredible intensity of them together, physically, but for the intimacy of that time in the cabin.

Aidan realized he was a man who had been given a gift worth cherishing. He had a sense of knowing where home was.

Not really in a cabin, or on a ranch. Not really in this brand-new home that they had designed and built together.

As beautiful as it was, this building was just a house. Home was where she was, where Noelle was. It was that place of safety where they laughed and cried and celebrated and felt sorrow together.

His home, forever, was nestled in the heart of the woman he loved.

"A purple one?" Tess asked.

"A purple what?"

He got *the* look.

"A purple hippopotamus, of course," Tess said.

"Yes, I think a purple hippopotamus would be perfect," Noelle agreed. He frowned at the wall. There were all kinds of logistics to consider. What size should it be? And who had the skill to paint a hippopotamus? It could just end up looking like a giant purple blob on the wall. Even if it turned out okay, did a hippopotamus of any color go with the carefully chosen nautical theme of the baby room at all?

But looking at his wife and his daughter, he knew none of that mattered. They weren't, either of them, about things looking perfect.

His daughter had tried so desperately to tell him that, when he had been busy giving her Christmases that looked so right, and felt so wrong.

Tess and Noelle were all about how things *felt*. Even if that was messy and chaotic and threw the best-laid plans to the wind.

He sighed, and decided not to weigh in on the hippopotamus. It was an argument he was bound to lose.

At that moment, the puppy, who was not allowed in here, pushed through the door. He was a black Lab, and he looked a lot like his namesake, Smiley, had.

Aidan had thought a puppy right now was the worst possible idea. But when Noelle and Tess were onside for something, they were a formidable pair.

The puppy, Smiley, too, thumped his tail, pleading to join them. Then in the excitement of having broken into the forbidden sanctum,

Smiley gave them an apologetic look and piddled on the floor.

And their laughter rang out and filled the room, and danced out the open windows and sparkled in the surrounding forest, like fairy dust.

Aidan, that most pragmatic of men, could picture that laughter taking on a life of its own, and going out and out and out from them. He could picture it threading its way around a Christmas wreath where he had seen the word *HOPE* and then soaring on, past the forest, over the glades, and beyond what he could see, and even beyond what he could imagine.

He could picture that laughter joining the rushing rivers and the shooting stars, joining the great mystery that had given birth to it in the first place.

Aidan, that most pragmatic of men, could picture the laughter holding a force within it as brilliant as sunlight, a force that radiated outward, the only force that had ever really changed the world.

Love.

Their laughter held the magnificent healing power of love.

* * * * *